Diary of a Sad Girl

Or, My Quest to Find Love on a Dying Planet

Nicole Levin

For Grandpa Bob

Author's Note

What you are about to read is my diary. Well, okay, it's adapted from my diary. It's fiction. Made up! But also based on real experiences and thoughts I've had.

This book was self-published. While I had many people texting me when they spotted errors, and Joule even did a pass at editing (thank you so much), there will be typos. I am sorry. I frequently consulted Strunk and White's *The Elements of Style,* but I still do not completely understand the semi-colon. Typos are a big part of who I am: a messy, imperfect human. Please forgive me for this.

That said, I can assure you that any mistakes will not interfere with the readability of this book. This book is very readable.

I have changed considerably since I wrote this book. The world has too. Most notably, I am less sad. Many times, while editing, I cringed at my character, Joelle, for being so depressed, or not knowing what I know now. But it felt dishonest to change things.

So, think of this book as a vessel. Think of it as reading your best friend's diary — from when she was going through a hard, transformative time.

And if you are going through a hard, transformative time — if you are struggling with work, existential anxiety, or dating during the apocalypse — know that you are not alone. Because that is why I ultimately chose to publish this book.

Because even though in many ways it's all getting so much worse, it gets better, too.

Part I

<u>Tuesday, November 27th, 2018</u>

Sometimes people ask me if I am sad.

I am

but aren't we all?

I am happy, too.

Sometimes.

———

I slept thirteen hours. This is a new record for me.

I don't need to be at work until ten. I debate walking to a cafe and buying my coworker a pastry – a fancy croissant or something. Her grandmother just died, and I have never seen her so sad. But it's gray outside, and I don't think the Los Angeles smog is good for my skin, so instead, I do a thirty-minute yoga video for weight loss.

The woman who teaches the video is named Leslie Fightmaster. Leslie tells me that I am beautiful and that I shouldn't be so hard on myself. I agree.

A pastry feels pretty dumb all things considered.

When I get to the Warner Brothers lot, I barrel past my peppy coworker Sam as he showers me with his typical morning greetings: "Good morning! How's it going?! I bought more oat milk! Did you see?!"

Sam is like a yellow lab — both in appearance and temperament: big, blonde, eager to please. He is always so happy, and I have always just been crying in my car.

I hide from him, often.

We are both assistants on a network television show about two cops that blow up a lot of things and are also best friends. Sam's job is to order and pick up lunch, and my job is to write down everything that the writers say. It's a lot of typing, and I may have developed tendinitis, so I have started occasionally wearing a wrist brace to work so that my coworkers know just how hard and fast I'm typing for them.

It's very possible that I got tendinitis from swiping so much on dating apps, but I do not tell them this.

The season is almost over, and we're on the final episode, which involves the love interest jumping out of a skyscraper with a bomb strapped to her wedding dress. My boss asked me to write a story area, a two-page document for the studio selling the themes and major storylines of our final episode. Other than the dress jumping, none of this has been finalized, so I use a few power words (culmination, what we do for love, etc.) and keep the rest vague.

This is technically the job of a staff writer, but I'm doing it without additional pay because it's a chance to prove myself. I'm not keeping track, but I think I've proven myself eleven times.

———

When I feel guilty for being unhappy at my job, I remind myself that Victor Frankel said that suffering is relative, and he survived the Holocaust.

———

At lunchtime, Sam arranges sixteen takeout salads (all in plastic containers) on the counter. They are arranged in order from the most important person on the show to the least (a perk of being an Executive Producer is that you get your lunch to the far left). My lunch is second from the right.

Sam smiles and greets us as we pick up our lunches. He is very good at his job. When I was the PA last season, I would just listen to podcasts about nuclear war, buy myself ice cream with the company card, and eat it in liquor store parking lots. Oh, how the writers loved having a Harvard graduate buying them coffee. For a while, I loved it too. "I don't think I'm too good for this," I told them, "I will do the grunt work."

We all eat lunch together in the big writers' room, the same room where we sit to pitch our fun cop ideas. The room is standard for a television show: dozens of chairs around a large mahogany table, walls covered in whiteboards,[1] a small window that won't open with a view of the parking lot.

We are in this room a lot.

Since most of the writers are wealthy men, our lunch conversations revolve around sports and real estate. I'm pretty good at pretending to know sports ("How about that Nick Foles?"), but I'm very bad at pretending to be able to afford a house.

Today, I walk to the cafeteria on the lot. I didn't order a salad. I tell people that it's because the place we ordered from uses plastic, and I'm trying to be environmental. But mostly I'm just trying to kill time.

———

Around five-thirty, Sam asks me if I want to stay and live tweet the East Coast premiere of the latest episode. I pretend like I can't hear him and go home. It's rare that I get to leave before six, and I'm trying to make it to the gym in time for "Insanity!" — a high intensity interval workout.

My gym is a dump, but it's only thirty dollars a month, and all of the workout classes are free (spin, yoga, etc.). I have worked very hard over the last four years to develop goodwill with the "Insanity!" instructor, Jade, an intense thirty-something brunette who works at

---

1. The boards are split into six columns, where we map out, in detail, acts one through six for each episode. Alexis, the other writers' assistant, also keeps a list of exercise goals for the room that we have long given up on: walk fifteen minutes a day, drink eight glasses of water, etc.

PETA and constantly posts on Facebook about how we are all bad people for benefiting from systemic racism.

One time she started class by announcing that we had gone to war with Syria, and it was the best workout of my life.

Today she points out that the whole front row of our class is vegan.

"Joelle, are you vegan?"

"I'm a vegetarian," I reply, kicking my knees up in a warmup jog.

"I'll give you this reusable straw if you promise to go vegan."

I look at the straw. It's metal and bendy and branded: "Happy Honda Days."

"Okay," I tell her, still jogging. I am a vegan now.

The burpees have done their job, and when I get home, I am too exhausted to care that society is on the brink of collapse. It's only 8 pm. I don't know what to do with all this time, so I message some boys on Hinge. They are all useless and out of town. I take a melatonin and go to sleep.

Before I close my eyes, I remind myself that this could be the night that the Big One hits.[2]

<u>Wednesday, November 28th, 2018</u>

I'm bored at work. I shop on Amazon for more melatonin.

Megan, a writer, stops me.

---

2. Geologists say that Southern California is overdue for a massive earthquake – 7.8 magnitude or larger – that will kill thousands and strand millions without help, since most of the roadways will collapse. I have been waiting for the Big One since I moved to Los Angeles and have luckily grown out of the phase in my life where I drunk-eat my earthquake supply kit.

"You know melatonin is pretty addictive, right?"

Megan is tall, blonde, and very wise. Her mom writes a newsletter about healthy eating, so she knows. I cancel my order. It's for the best. Amazon is problematic anyway, even if I can't explain why.

"Are you working on your pilot?"

Another producer, Trey, is now hovering over my computer — one drawback to having a desk in the middle of the hallway. He's got long hair and Bradley Cooper vibes.

"Yes."

"You know this downtime is really rare. It's a gift. Soon we'll all be working sixty-hour weeks again. You should make the most of this, write something good."

Trey is writing a short film, a screenplay, and maybe something for the Chinese.

"You should write a memoir," Patrick, a mid-level writer, joins in.

I have always wanted to write a book. In fact, the reason I went into television was so that I could eventually write some sort of tell-all *Bossy Pants*-esque dive into my childhood once I got successful enough to warrant it. But given both the structure of the entertainment world and scientists' projections for the actual one, I no longer think that I have enough time to achieve success first.

I do not tell Patrick this. Instead, I tell Patrick that a memoir is presumptuous: I'm just another white girl who read a lot of Vonnegut during her formative years. Lena Dunham exists. My voice has been heard.

"Besides," I say. "Where do I start?"

He considers. "Why don't you write about your favorite food: grapes? You eat so many. Why?"

He puts his fists in his pockets, stretching the lining of his sweatshirt.

"Grapes have lots of sugar, and sugar is addictive."

"But why grapes?" he asks, "Are they a metaphor for something deeper?"

I tell him that I will think about this, but secretly I'm incensed. Who is he to comment on my eating habits?

———

I eat some grapes and think about it. Is there something deeper going on here? I started eating a lot of grapes when Trump was elected. But I was eating grapes before then, too.

———

After work, I make plans with one of the useless Hinge boys to see a movie. It's the third date, and I think he's not trying as hard to impress me, because when I ask if he'll pick me up, he tells me he'll give me a ride home. I know what he's trying to do, but I don't tell him I'm onto him.

I call my mom in the Uber. She's watching *Outlander* with my dad, but she pauses the TV to talk to me. My Bubbie used to say that your mother is your best friend, and on some days, I believe it.

"Where are you off to?" she asks.

"To see a movie." I try to keep things as vague as possible. My mom doesn't approve of "app dating." She thinks that I should meet someone in person like my brother did. But all I do is work and exercise, where would I meet someone? The gym? My membership is only $30 dollars a month. I cannot risk the one good thing in my life.

"Why don't you date your coworker, Gideon?" She is constantly suggesting that I date Gideon because he is tall and nice.

"I know he's perfect, but he has a girlfriend."

"You know, you can't be so picky."

———

I spot the Hinge boy immediately. He looks like a young Steve Buscemi: small, gentle face, poor posture. I have not figured him out yet. He works at NPR, lives with his parents, and drives a Camaro. The Camaro makes me very uneasy: what is he compensating for? He's being very loud in the Arclight lobby, going on about something that I don't care about.

I shush him. "Movie theater voices."

"I don't think that's a thing," he says.

"I have a reputation to maintain."

My date seems agitated, hyper. He makes a fuss about buying my ticket, so I offer to buy us popcorn. I want a large popcorn for obvious reasons (I've only eaten salad today), but he seems to think a small is enough. I don't press the issue because I don't want to shatter any illusions of my femininity.

The movie is good, and my date does a good job of both not touching my thigh too much and laughing at what I believe to be the more feminist jokes in the movie. We do not have enough popcorn.

As we exit, I see my roommate and his girlfriend a few yards ahead of us. It's too much work to introduce everyone, so I pull my date back behind a trash can. "My roommate can't meet you." He is surprisingly cool with this.

I make him hide again when I bring him to my apartment — a rather spacious two-bedroom two-bath in Los Feliz,[3] a neighborhood just east of Hollywood. I like my apartment and my neighborhood, and I have lived in the same three-mile radius for nearly five years. When I first moved to Los Feliz, someone told me it was "wannabe Brooklyn" because we had cute shops and an independent movie theater, and everyone was a hipster. That sounded perfect to me.

"Do you want a drink?" I ask once we enter. My living room is large — there is a couch and a chair — but we cannot take up space here. I grab him one of two Bud Lights left

---

3. Pronounced "Los Fee-Les" because at this point even the Spanish language has been gentrified.

over from some social event I can't remember and make him stay in my room. I don't want my roommate — who I have known for eight years — to think I'm a harlot.[4]

We make out for a little bit, and then he asks me if I want to "bang." Now, I'm really in my head about harloting. I think about what choices I must have made to end up here, sitting on top of a 27-year-old boy who is too loud and uses the word "bang" to describe sex.

"I need a second." I take a swig from his beer.

He is confused, and possibly emasculated, so I try to explain the Madonna-Whore complex to him so that he understands where I'm coming from. It turns out that I do not really know the Madonna-Whore complex, so I end up just drinking more beer and pointing to a stack of books I keep alongside my bed.

"Are you turned on by my stack of books?"

"No. I'm turned on by your naked body."

I give up and make out with him more, but we do not "bang" because I have broken his spirit. He is limp.

It's raining outside, so I offer him a trash bag to cover his head. Before he leaves, I give him one last chance to admire my books.

"That's Joan Didion. She's really good."

———

---

4. I'm not a harlot. Not that inviting a boy into your home makes you a harlot, or that there is anything wrong with harloting in general. I imagine one day I will be older and more confident about these kinds of things, but for now that day seems far off.

Thursday, November 29th, 2018

Cheyenne is in town for a night. She's one of my best friends from college who currently lives in D.C. Our long-distance relationship is very strong (I call her almost daily), but we don't really travel well together. I'm type A; she is a free spirit. I once heard a story about her being three hours late to something involving a rental car, so I'm worried that this visit will destroy us.

However, I'm not so worried that I offer to pick her up from the airport, even though she is flying into Bob Hope, a notoriously painless airport located just ten minutes from my work.

Instead, I go to the gym. I remind myself that I can't take care of others if I don't take care of myself first.

After a short run on the treadmill, I feel increasingly guilty about not picking up Cheyenne, so I go to Trader Joe's and buy her a welcome snack. How can she be mad at me when I bought her all these snap peas to dip in hummus?

She can't. When she finally arrives, she's starving. She picks from the spread as she tells me about how her flight from San Francisco was delayed five hours.

"It was a forty-minute flight, I could have driven in that time." Cheyenne examines a pita chip methodically before biting into it.

We studied the same thing in college – government, with a minor in energy and the environment – but Cheyenne is very different from me. Whereas I am short and unsure and brunette, Cheyenne is tall and confident and blonde – very Aryan. She works in solar energy and climbs rocks for fun. She's hooked up with women.

"Sorry for not picking you up."

"No, this is great. I haven't eaten all day."

I have never not eaten all day.

———

I take Cheyenne to the Dresden, a bar in my neighborhood full of old Hollywood and bad jazz. My roommate, Paul, is with us. He slouches over his Moscow mule. Paul is very smart, and he's constantly using words that I don't understand, even in context. We do not hang out often.

"This is where they filmed *Swingers*," I tell Cheyenne.

"What is *Swingers*?"

"Some movie from the sixties."

My roommate corrects: "It's from the 90s."

Embarrassed and eager to change the subject, I offer to buy a round of overpriced cocktails. Cheyenne accepts.

Cheyenne asks Paul what he does for a living, and I am surprised to learn that he is now editing content for a robot Instagram influencer. I did not know he had a job, nor did I know that robots used Instagram.

He shows us her (its?) profile, which reads: "19 forever, Black Lives Matter, Robot." She has millions of followers. It is very dystopian.

"They get models to pose in the clothing and then they animate the body. She's all AI."

We drink.

When we got drunk in college Cheyenne used to steal things. I remember crashing a European party on the fifth floor of Ridgely Hall (the apartment complex next to Insomnia Cookies) and her coming down the stairs after with a pair of Hunter boots.

"Someone left these outside their door!" she explained. "Can you believe it?"

"Cheyenne, you have to put those back!"

Now, Cheyenne hands me her drink – something with whiskey and pineapple. "Try this, it's incredible."

I sip it, probably too fast. It's very good. Because I am worried that Paul is left out of the drink sharing, I tell him that I saw him at the movie theater yesterday.

"I made my date hide from you because he looked like Steve Buscemi."

"Oh, we saw you come home," says my roommate. "We waited outside for a couple minutes so that you wouldn't be uncomfortable."

"Oh."

"Yeah."

I offer to buy him another drink. He declines.

Friday, November 30, 2018

I get to work on time but hungover, so I drown myself in coffee. We spend the first two hours of work talking about the relative merits of Los Angeles versus New York.

My boss would never live in New York, but Patrick thinks conversations are more interesting on the East Coast. Everyone here just works in entertainment, whereas in New York there is a diversity of professions.

When my boss remembers that we have real work, we spend the next seven hours straight rebreaking the final episode.[5] I work through lunch and furiously type everything down, organizing as I go.

When I leave work at seven, I'm broken.

---

5. Rebreak [verb]: A very common phenomenon in television where you take a completed episode and then haphazardly change everything. We like to do it at least three times per episode, the final script usually resembling the original plot we started with.

Sunday, December 2, 2018

Dream log: I discover that my boss is my biological father. I have two dads now.

———

Monday, December 3, 2018

I'm worried that I'm getting sick, so at work, I take a DayQuil and then eat some Emergent-C straight from the pouch.

Megan is alarmed: "That's how people die!" She's right. I almost choke.

I'm flirting so much with death lately.

Trey pulls me into his office and asks me if I want to help him rewrite his script, *Drunk U*. It's a feature about a failing liberal arts college and an alcoholic professor who teaches uptight students to party in order to get admissions up and save the school.

"I want the tone to be like *Atlanta*," he says. "Or maybe *Eighth Grade*." I try to keep a straight face.

"I'll pay you $350 a week."

I nod my head and tell Trey that this is a good idea.

Trey also wonders why I have been so silent for the last few weeks in the writers' room.

"You used to pitch so much; you were really killing it for a while."

I shrug.

Last month, I got scolded twice in one day. First by a senior writer who told me that I was laughing too much at his pitches, and later by Patrick, who was upset that I didn't back him up when he was standing up for the female characters in the show.

"They are all props," he ranted, "designed to support the male character's storylines. They have no desires or wants of their own."

I sat quietly as the older men on the show pushed back about how this was not true. The female characters all had jobs and careers; how could they be props? Besides, even if they are props, this show is not about women, it's about two cops that are also best friends.

———

Even though I'm kind of sick, I send Buscemi boy a text. He had said some really nice things about how he was happy I'm alive still, so I'm under the (potentially misguided) assumption that he wants to see me again.

A low bar, I know.

I send him a picture of the stack of books by my bed.

Me: Are you into these?

BB: I can't see the spines! Those could be junie b jones books for all I know.

I'm making this so easy for him. Why can't he just play along? And what's wrong with *Junie B. Jones*?

———

Tuesday, December 4, 2018

On the way to work I catch some of NPR's *Take 2*. I really hate the host, Adolfo Martinez. He's always saying things like "Happy Friday!" on days when the world is ending. Today he tells us what to pack in our "Go Bags" in case of another fire.

After my parents almost lost their house in the Tick Fire, I started keeping rations in my car and my tank at half-full. I thought I was prepared, but apparently, I also need duct tape. Adolfo won't tell me why, exactly, but he cryptically alludes to the fact that we'll definitely need it for something.

There's not much going on at work, so I spend most of the morning trying to log back into my mom's Amazon Prime so that I can buy duct tape (and melatonin). It takes me a couple of attempts before I can remember her password and by then I've triggered some sort of security alert. I give up. I'm boycotting Amazon officially now.

My boss leaves early, and I sneak out after him.

I thought the nine-to-five was a myth, but here it is, finally I'm living it, and it's amazing.

Before Thanksgiving I had been working sixty hours a week, sometimes even seventy. The first all-nighter I ever pulled was for this show. For episode 213, we stayed until 11 pm breaking the story. I drove home tired and then turned the fifty pages of notes I'd taken into something coherent by the next morning. (I also had to write pages of the script, manage phones, and reply to emails for my boss.)

This happened regularly for a few months. It was fun at first. I felt special getting to stay up late with these talented writers, getting to even write words that showed up on television. But eventually, I got sick of it. Felt used. When would my name appear in the credits? Next season? No. The season after that?

I never got an episode of my own, but my boss bought me a pair of Uggs once.

———

I get to "Insanity!" and hide in the back because I've learned from Facebook that Jade is now doing a no-plastic thing, and I'm scared that if I stand in the front row, she will pressure me into giving that up, too. I'm not ready to give up plastic yet. There is too much free food at work.

After ninety minutes of jumping around (I stayed for core class), I lay down on a blue mat in the corner and pretend to stretch. I'm still trying to get Buscemi boy to take the hint about hanging out, but he's gone on some tangent about the young adult detective series *Encyclopedia Brown*. It's not great banter, so, high on endorphins from all my jumping around, I finally get to the point and ask him if he wants to hang out this week.

When he finally responds, it's only to tell me that work is really crazy. He has to wake up at 5am on Thursday. He asks about next week and then makes a comment about how detective novels featuring a strong female lead are the real mystery to him.

He is dead to me.

I wait an appropriate amount of time (two hours) and then tell him that I'm free next week.

—

Wednesday, December 5, 2018

Most of the workday is spent discussing where we should hold this year's holiday dinner. We brainstorm a list of expensive restaurants on one of the whiteboards.

I get a text from another Hinge boy who I went on a couple of dates with in November. He's from Kansas, and that might be the most distinctive thing about him. Kansas got really drunk on our second date and told me that climate change wasn't the leading cause of the wildfires in California. This was back when I had taken to wearing a mask to deal with all the smoke in the air, so I was extra sensitive. I told him that there would be no third date, but he must have thought I was joking, because he's been texting me twice a week for the last month. He keeps sending me question marks, as if more punctuation will change how I feel about him.

Kansas: Are you free this weekend?

Kansas: Also, if you're not interested in hanging out, that's okay too.

Kansas: ?

Kansas: ??

None of my subtle non-responses are working, so I text him that I'm not in the mental place to date. A guy told me this once after a first date, and even though I'm still a little miffed about it (why didn't he tell me before I bought the $15.99 Miranda July book he recommended?), I think it's a good line.

It works. Kansas thanks me for my honesty and tells me that he will be here waiting for when I become less mental and am ready to date again.

———

Thursday, December 6, 2018

Dream Log: I'm dating Cheyenne. We try out lesbian sex, and I don't really like it. Maybe because in the dream world lesbian sex consists of sitting on someone's lap with jeans on.

Outside, El Niño is happening. The rain falls from my gutters in sheets. It's torrential, probably carrying garbage and oil from the streets out into the ocean. I cannot go back to sleep.

I'm too upset about Buscemi boy. I'm also upset at me for being upset about a dumb boy I don't even like.

I'm on the brink of unemployment, carbon emissions are rising, and my grandpa has cancer. Why am I upset about a boy? I have so many better things to be sad about.

I write all this down, and then I make a vow to never be upset with this boy again. I go back to sleep and dream about being naked at work.

———

It's another slow day. I sneak into a side office and watch *Riverdale* on one of the extra generic black couches.[6] I need human connection but don't want to get up, so I call my brother Michael who lives in D.C. He's three years older than me, but people used to think that we were twins because we talked so much and hung out all the time. He was a good older brother. During his senior year of high school, he sat me down and planned out the next four years of my high school life. "You will skip PE, double up on sciences sophomore year, and be valedictorian."

I did. I was.

We were both in zero-period leadership, and sometimes, at 6 am, as he drove me to school, he would close his eyes, throw his hands up and scream, "Jesus take the wheel!"

---

6. I like Riverdale because I can generally turn my brain off while watching.

It's been a few weeks since we last spoke, he's been busy with his new job in the federal government and his upcoming wedding.

"Do you think I need to invite the Friedmans?" he asks. "We invited too many people, but they were always there for me, you know?"

I tell him that he should just elope.

———

After lunch, I still don't want to write, so I go on Bumble. I stopped using Bumble because all the men on it looked like male models and the app makes the woman message the guy first (somehow this is more feminist?). I am very lazy, and men are infinite, so I prefer that they message me first. But Hinge has gotten very sad (still not as sad as Tinder), and every guy either seems desperate for a relationship or too eager to bone.

A lot of men are on both apps, though, and as I swipe I re-match with a few I've matched with before. I send a "heyyyy" to the guy with the long hair I ghosted on J-Swipe. Maybe he'll be less boring on this user interface.

He's not.

I swipe and swipe and swipe. I cannot tell if I'm looking for a diversion or if I'm looking for love. At this point, I would take either. I have never really had a proper boyfriend (a product of both overachieving in high school and hookup culture in college), and I think I might like to find someone before society crumbles and we're living in a Cormac McCarthy novel. It'd be nice to have someone to pull me out of the rubble.

I swipe some more. I match with a boy who looks cool and sad (he's playing the guitar on stage in one picture). His profile says that he's looking for a girl with two kidneys, so I message him.

Me: My kidneys are v hot

He likes this.

———

At the gym, I stress-run five miles because all the TVs are set to *CNN*. I cannot see the screens, but I can sense that bad things are happening.

Sometimes, I think that when people die, it will mean that there are fewer carbon emissions and that this will be better for the environment (me) in the long term. I only ever think this for a second, because I remind myself that it's selfish and wrong and that the people dying are not the people emitting, and even if they were, this is not how the science works. This is eco-fascism.

I worry about what will happen to me when I become resource scarce.

———

Friday, December 7, 2018

Dream Log: I spoke Chinese at some point, but not well.

———

Alexis, the other writer's assistant, is mad at me. She asked me for a gym recommendation, and then I asked her if she was working out for the new boy she met on Bumble.

"You were being too sassy," she tells me from behind a massive computer screen. "I want to work out for myself." Alexis is very confident and from Baltimore. I suspect that she holds grudges.

I apologize profusely. I did not mean what I said. I do not think sometimes. She's still upset, so I hide in another room and then text her an invitation to a party that I technically wasn't invited to.

Me: This will be fun. It's witch themed

She does not respond.

———

When I get to "Insanity!" I want to stand in the front, so I tell Jade that I'm going to give up plastic when my TV show ends. She does not seem as excited for me as I think she should be, but she tells me where I can get refillable soap.

———

I have plans to go to a holiday party for an alumni association that I'm only marginally involved with – Harvardwood. It's supposed to connect Harvard alumni in entertainment with other alumni in entertainment.

I met my coworker Megan in a Harvardwood pilot-writing workshop, where I wrote a mediocre script about quarantining on a cruise ship during a pandemic. I remember thinking that we would never have been friends in college because she played soccer and was tall.

Out of school, we became friends. One time while getting drinks, she mentioned that her show was looking for an assistant. That's how I got my job.[7]

It is not lost on me that I was privileged to even hear about, much less lock down a job delivering lunch and coffee.

Megan is not going to this party, but another friend of mine – Casey – is. Casey is tall and strong and sometimes unhinged. We met in undergrad, and we were friends because neither of us played sports and we were on the same comedy magazine, *The Harvard Lampoon*. We are very similar, but I'm better about texting than she is. She has just cut her hair very short, and I tell her that it looks great on her, because it does.

It's at a bar in Hollywood, the Parlor, in a side room that is too loud and smells faintly of stale dreams. Everyone here is aspiring: aspiring writers, aspiring producers, aspiring directors, aspiring actors. It is a lot of networking – forced smiles. Yes, we are all working hard now – as assistants, waiters, tutors, writing on the side – but it will pay off. Any day now, any day.

---

7. The interview (with my now-boss) mostly consisted of him repeatedly asking: "You know that this job is just getting lunch, right?" and me assuring him that I was fine with that.

One man who used to be in my writers' workshop comes up and asks me what I'm working on now. He loves the script I wrote about the aliens.[8] Have I written anything since? It's been a whole year.

"Sorry, I need to get a drink."

I need to get multiple drinks, it turns out. Tequila sodas.

The pressure of advancing my sad career dissipates with my sobriety. I can't network when I'm tipsy. It is just a normal party now. My mood has improved drastically.

Casey sees her old roommate, and we all end up talking to an attractive assistant director from Birmingham. He's somewhat stout, with great skin and a wide smile. It's going well, but then he mentions he's been casually seeing this girl who works for Gal Gadot. I cannot compete with a girl who works for a model.

I want to seem unavailable and aloof, so I tell him how I took this guy who looked like Steve Buscemi back to my place and made him look at my books. I realize — probably around the Steve Buscemi reference — that this is not a good story to tell someone I want to seduce, but I'm already so far in that if I don't finish the story, it won't make sense.

"I kicked him out of my apartment immediately."

After a couple more minutes of conversation, the boy hands me his business card.

"I'm going to Atlanta for three months, but when I get back let's connect."

As we leave, Casey turns to me: "You're soulmates."

I do not disagree.

When I get home, I cook some vegan meatballs from Trader Joe's and take a melatonin. These are probably the last vegan meatballs I will ever eat because the packaging is plastic.

---

8. In which former lead singer of Blink-182 Tom Delonge moves in with my family in Fairfield and pulls a young girl -- lost and fresh out of college -- into an alien conspiracy.

Saturday, December 8, 2018

After a haircut, a shower, and a series of Ubers, I arrive at a fundraising party for the Harvard Lampoon. The party is at the Jonathan Club.

The venue is terrifying. There is a statue of Reagan in the lobby, and some of the televisions in the lounge are set to Russian news. It reeks of mac 'n' cheese and privilege. There are a lot of white men.

Last year, my show's Christmas special took place at the Jonathan Club (we changed the name for legal reasons). In the episode, the president of the club worked with a ring of white nationalists to smuggle meth into Los Angeles via a denim company.

We were not so off-base. White supremacy, white nationalism, where do you draw the line, really?

It took me a long time to get on the Lampoon. Many – very funny – people at Harvard never did. The magazine was legendary – after college, staff went off to write for *Saturday Night Live*, *The Simpsons*, *Conan*, and *Parks and Rec*. (I got my first job out of college because I had Lampoon on my LinkedIn).[9] Getting onto the magazine was seen as objective proof that you are funny.

The Lampoon building – known as "The Castle" – was mysterious. It was a funny-looking red brick building in the middle of Mount Auburn Street, right by Adams House and the Hillel. Its windows and door made a face.

Unless you were on the Lampoon staff (or a graduating senior), no one was allowed upstairs in the building. There were often parties in the Castle, with celebrities: Bryan Cranston, Tina Fey, Katy Perry. I walked by one day to see the Harlem Globetrotters playing a basketball game in the street.

------

9. I also got two cat-sitting jobs from alumni connections.

It felt like the coolest and most exclusive place on campus. The magazine was the arbiter of who was funny. I *was* funny, but without their stamp of approval, I didn't think that I was.

I had to get on.

I spent two and a half years trying.

The process of trying out, "comping," consisted of bringing in printed comedy pieces for feedback twice a week. Since no one was allowed upstairs, all the "compers" were relegated to the first-floor library. It was a cramped circular room with no chairs, so we all sat on the floor, on a worn-out, beer-stained burgundy carpet. (I spent hours in college ironing off candle wax from this carpet.) My feet always fell asleep by the time it was my turn to talk to one of the two "Comp Directors" who would give me feedback.

I remember the Lampoon information session I attended freshman fall. Dozens of students packed into that room while the Comp Directors, in suits and ties, walked us through the process of getting on: submissions in 12 pt. font, three rounds of cuts, and a name-blind vote by the entire staff in the final round. They could take none of us or all of us.

"Comp" stood for competition. The process was hyper-competitive. That night the library was filled with thirty- or forty-people, young students, mostly boys. This was one of six meetings. Hundreds of students tried to get on the magazine each semester, for literature (writing), art, and the infamous business comp (which consisted of selling hundreds of thousands of dollars in ads for our magazine). Five to twelve would get on.

I did not feel like I was competing with these other boys – I was competing with the few women who wanted to get on. Yes, the process was in theory "name-blind." But I had never seen them take more than one woman from the literature comp.

The information sessions all had pranks. The premise of the prank at my first information session involved a party happening in another room. Loud music boomed from behind a door and a tall upperclassman keep barging into the library and interrupting the Comp Directors, each time more drunk and less clothed. It culminated with him topless, in boxers, with his penis sticking out. A condom was on it, and he picked it off and flung it into the crowd. It landed on my foot. I was wearing sandals. This was the first penis I saw at Harvard.[10]

I was eighteen. I was a virgin. I did not think I belonged here.

But I came back to *The Lampoon*, semester after semester, each time getting one round closer to getting on. I was ashamed, about everything: my sexual inexperience, my softness, the fact that I had failed at something, failed at getting in.

And I was thriving in my other extracurriculars: the school newspaper *The Crimson*, the comedy satire news show. But this was not enough: anyone could write for those publications.

Over time the comp slowly changed who I was. I learned to be like the men that ran the competition: aloof, absurd, elitist.

That's funny," I began saying instead of laughing. I tried to laugh; it did not sound the same. I began to cackle, loud and goose-like. More performative than sincere.

My sophomore spring, I made it to the final round of cuts. During the cocktail party (which also always involved a gag[11]) they took me into a side room filled with dozens of men and candles and asked me a series of questions: "Crimson or Lampoon," "Nick or Thomas." Perhaps it was meant to be playful, but Thomas was perched right behind me. I could feel his crotch behind my head.

These men were all so strange to me. Some of them were in my dorm, but they were never around. I saw Thomas once in my dining hall, and while I was piling my plate with lettuce, he told me not to give up, to comp again.

---

10. I later found out that this man was accused of sexual assault while at Harvard (in the Lampoon, during a party) and gave the graduation speech anyways.

11. They hired an Obama impersonator one semester, brought a bunch of farm animals inside another. One semester, a woman was paid to give haircuts and – because the party was ending, and I didn't think I was allowed to stay – I drunkenly ran out of the Castle with only half my hair done. After the compers were gone, the staff writers would wrestle in the library.

I knew these boys were fucked up, but I fell in love with them and never told them. One by one I let them break my heart.

———

Late on a Sunday in November my junior year, they knocked on my door and told me that I did not get on.

They handed me an envelope with my pieces – covered in insults – and a page of legal jargon explaining Massachusetts hazing law. Then they left. Before I could connect the dots, they ran back up the stairs and pounded on the door.

"Get on your knees, fool," they yelled at me. They gave me a dunce hat and a purple shirt that spelled "Phool." I signed a contract agreeing that by Massachusetts law this was not hazing.

The weekend was a mix of horror and magic. They made me skip around campus and sing some song about "Cunnilingus" every time I crossed the street. I was handed a speech about the Marathon Bombing – mocking both the recent terrorism and my column in *The Crimson*. I was supposed to memorize it. I did.

They took us to Mount Auburn Cemetery and made us dance on the graves. "What is the meaning of the *Harvard Lampoon*?" They asked us time and time again. Every answer we gave was wrong. Other than one presentation about the coffee industry that I gave with Cheyenne, reeking of cigarette smoke, I did not go to class for a week. I barely slept. In my spare time, I memorized the millions of lyrics to silly made-up songs and the poems they told me to learn. They took me to a gun range in New Hampshire. They flew another kid to New York for lunch.

They told us that we were not on the magazine yet. We still had to prove ourselves to the graduate board – a group of alums coming to judge us. I believed them.

I felt insane. This was the best and worst week of my life. The attention was magical. The days surreal. They bought us burritos and ice cream. They took the four female phools down to the basement and gave us cake and champagne. "It's hard to be a woman on staff," someone had said, "we need to stick together. Connect."

They asked us about our first kisses, about embarrassing moments, when we lost our virginity. I did not trust them. But it also felt nice to share. I let my guard down because I was sleep deprived.

Two hours later, the entire staff joined back up, and all our secrets were used as material for jokes against us. The very men who I loved and feared mocked us, persistently, until 5 am. I sat panicked on that carpet, now soiled with melted wax and crumbs, waiting for all these men to make fun of my virginity. They never did. It took me years to trust these women again.

I never once thought about walking away. The initiation process was, as I later found out, "completely optional."

On Thursday night – after a long day of sitting around in a basement convinced that I had been black-balled – they walked me up a spiral staircase to the top of the Castle. They opened a window overlooking a massive hall. There was a large table, candle chandeliers, absurd art, plates, drawings, masks, all hanging on the wall.

Someone dressed as a jester sang me a limerick, and dozens of staff and alum threw wet sponges at me.

When I got down to the room, the people who had tortured me for a week hugged me and lifted me onto a big wooden table to dance. They handed me a bottle of champagne and a plate stolen from Adams Dining Hall. Mine to throw off the table and break. I had finally gotten on the *Harvard Lampoon*.

Vanitas, they taught us. Nothing matters. There is no meaning to the Lampoon.

I thought it would be gone after that, the feeling of having to prove myself, the culture of mocking and being mocked.

It never ended. These boys became my best friends, and the meanest people I would ever know. The most privileged people I would ever know. I became loud and obnoxious, and for many years I believed that humor was the goal, not a tool to use for something greater. Because there was no meaning.

But on that night, I was so happy.

———

I am less happy at this party. The magic has long worn off, and I'm forced to donate when I arrive. There is an open bar, and I think that I can drink fifty dollars' worth of alcohol.

I cannot.

Even though most of the writers have high-profile jobs, no one seems content. No one has really made it — no, not yet.

By seven, I have drunk all that I can (two tequila sodas) and eaten all that I could (nothing, there were no vegan options) and consequently I'm very drunk. At one point a tall thirty-something alum who looks like Charlie Day flirts with me and touches my arm, but he leaves before asking for my number.

I wonder what I am doing here.

———

Sunday, December 9th, 2018

I wake up hungover with regret: How much money did I spend on Uber? Why did I add that guy who touched my arm on Facebook? Why hasn't he added me back?

As punishment, I force myself to walk two miles to yoga. I listen to music along the way and reflect on how beautiful Los Angeles is on cold winter days. I don't let myself enjoy it though (because of climate change) and remind myself that this is all temporary. Soon the air will be unbreathable. It will be hot every day.

I stop by the farmer's market in the Wells Fargo parking lot, at the refillable soap station Jade mentioned. It's a tent with dozens of giant pumps full of conditioner, shampoo, detergent, dish soap. I buy a glass container full of shampoo and some mesh produce bags and fill my empty plastic Pantene bottle with conditioner. The total is over forty dollars.

"That can't be right?"

The cashier shrugs.

I walk home with my backpack full of heavy glass.

———

When I get back, my roommate is hunched over a PlayStation Portable at the kitchen table, and since it has been weighing on me for quite a while, I finally ask him if he's prepared for the Big One.

"I have an earthquake supply kit, but I don't really want to have to share it with you. Do you have any rations?"

"No, but don't worry, if the earthquake hits, I'll just jump into the crevasse."

———

I have a date, with the organ harvester from Bumble. We've been texting a lot lately — a mistake, I think. Boys never live up to the fictional version I create in my head. I once got so excited about a date over text — cute, funny, went to Harvard — and when I met him my face visibly fell. His voice was too high.

I think that this will probably be the case with kidney man, too. I try not to get too excited. He will have a funny voice, I tell myself. It will not work out.

He's already at the Dresden when I arrive, sitting at a corner booth, nursing a drink to calm his nerves. I realize I have forgotten my date's real name, which is not unusual for me. I discreetly check Bumble. It's Jesse.

It still seems weird to use his name, so I slide into the booth and tell him this is the bar where *Swingers* was filmed.

He shakes his head; he's never seen it.

Real Jesse does not quite line up with Fictional Jesse. In my head, he is loud and ironic and has long hair. In person, he is soft-spoken and sincere. His hair is short, but I was prepared for this because he texted to warn me that he had a bad haircut. He has big teeth and reminds me of Zach Woods.

I make a joke about how it seems like he always has a library voice — appropriate because he is studying to become a librarian — and he gets anxious.

"This is the way my voice sounds. I can't change it. I can try to talk louder if you want."

"That's okay," I say. "I just want a drink."

"What do you want?"

"I'll go with you," I insist. "I would like the bartender to hand me the drink directly." Just in case he was serious about the kidneys.

I order the drink Cheyenne got last time we were here and watch as Jesse pulls out his credit card. "I'm sorry for not pretending to reach for my wallet." This is my new move.

"It's okay, I'm only selectively poor," he says.

"Are you selectively rich?"

"I'm not."

We return to the table, and I pull out my reusable "Happy Honda Days" straw. I make a joke to ease the tension: "I was worried about running out of conversation, so I brought a prop."

He lights up in excitement and pulls down his shirtsleeve, revealing a list of discussion topics written on the inside of his forearm in Sharpie: "I was worried about that, too!"

His handwriting is bad, so it takes me a moment to read all the crazy things he's written on his skin. And they are crazy: cymatics, fantasy racism, UFOs, conspiracy theories. What kind of person needs a reminder to talk about UFOs?

I am uneasy. By societal standards, this boy is past the point of eccentric and bordering on insane. I should get up and leave, probably, before I am abducted, drawn into some sort of counterculture incongruous with my current life.

But on the other hand, society is broken. Our quest for societally acceptable lives has destroyed the planet, marginalized millions, threatened humanity.

I stay put.

"What is cymatics?" I ask.

"It's a vibrational phenomenon. Here, I'll look it up for you." He pulls out his phone and shows me some images of waves on Google. "I don't actually have much else to say about them, I just think they're pretty."

"They're not really a great conversation topic then, are they?"

"I guess not."

I drink.

"Do you want to talk about something else on the list? Conspiracy theories?" He is desperate.

I want this to work out for some reason, maybe because I'm not ready to let the fictional version of him die, so I throw him a bone. "You said you were working on an album. What's it about?"

He smiles, "Satan."

Well, I tried.

He starts to tell me how he's gotten really into Satanism recently, but because so many alarm bells are going off in my head, I miss his explanation of what this entails.

"Sorry, I zoned out. Can you repeat that?"

It turns out he's just interested in reading about Satan in literature (his favorite depiction is in the Koran), and he does not believe he (or she!) exists, nor does he worship Satan.

"If Satan were real, he would like ABBA."

I wish Megan or Alexis were here — I'd like a second opinion.

"Are you going to murder me?" I ask.

"I don't like that you keep asking that."

I don't trust him, but my mom has also told me that I am too mean to men, so I apologize for assuming the worst. He tells me it's fine. He works with seventh graders. They're worse. They make fun of the way he walks.

I have to pee, so I chug my drink (because I'm still worried about leaving it unattended) and head to the bathroom. I check my phone in the stall, but I have no updates or new matches. And the flirty boy from last night has still not accepted my friend request.

When I get back to the booth, I'm drunk and sad. I have also stolen a handful of dinner mints from the restaurant portion of the bar, so I eat them one by one as I confess to Jesse that I don't understand why anyone is doing what they are doing, given the information we all have.

"What do you mean?"

"The world is ending."

I think he is sad now, too, because how could he not be?

"What else is on your arm?"

"Conspiracy theories?"

"I don't want to talk about that."

I'm intrigued. I don't want the night to end, so when he suggests we go on a walk to look for neighborhood cats, I agree. I assume it's some sort of ploy to make out on the sidewalk (or murder me, I guess).

We leave The Dresden and wander around some cottages in Los Feliz. When it becomes apparent that he's not plotting to do either – he just loves cats, and his just died of AIDS — I tell him that it's too cold and suggest we go eat at a well-lit diner a few blocks away. He agrees.

I watch him walk. He is tall and skinny and moves only using his legs, but the seventh graders are wrong: his gait is the least weird thing about him.

We sit in another booth, this one with better lighting, and I order vegan tacos. He pays, even though he doesn't order because he has some illogical justification for spending all his money. He is a socialist. The more he spends the less he lets money consume him, he tells me.

"Did you donate to Yemen?" I ask, virtue signaling. "I donated to Yemen."

He seems confused. He brings up a Peter Singer article about maximizing donations.

"I already bought mosquito nets," I tell him. "I read that article in college."

I'm so proud of myself for being smart, but he doesn't seem so impressed.[12]

I go through his wallet and look for evidence that he is who he says he is. He tries to hide a Dungeons and Dragons membership card but proudly hands me his Arkansas ID. He tells me that he used to look like a Tsarnaev brother. Maybe this is a relic from my college hazing, but it's not a bad look.

His leg grazes mine, and maybe it's just the tacos, but excitement shoots down my leg. I am attracted to him. But I can't tell if that's because I'm so lonely and sad, or because he's cute.

I look at him. His face is pale and childish. Somewhat sickly. He looks anemic. I remember about the kidneys. Maybe he's dying. He's either dying or going to murder me for my organs or both.

"Are you dying?"

"No."

I let him walk me home.

As we walk, I give him tips for online dating so that he can have more success with the next one. He shouldn't text girls so much before meeting them. He shouldn't bring up Satanism so early in the night. He shouldn't write conversation topics on his arm – or, if he does, he should write topics that are more interesting to women, questions that invite

---

12. I actually have no idea what I'm talking about, but I vaguely recall reading his article for a philosophy class in college and then donating $80 to a mosquito net/anti-malaria foundation.

them to talk about themselves and their experiences: *Where are you from? What do you do?* etc. And he should do a better job at hiding them.

I feel bad for saying all this, so I double back and tell him that I'm wrong and that he should not change (I am not trying to change him!) and maybe one day he will meet a girl (or boy!) who likes him for who he is.

"Just be yourself!"

"I've gotten this advice before."

When we get to my building, he mentions that he used to live on this street, and he was friends with an old woman in the building next to me.

"Is she still alive?" he asks.

"I don't know. She went to elementary school with Hitler."

He starts to tell me something, but because I'm wondering about whether or not cat AIDS can spread to people, I miss the story about young Hitler. I do not ask him to repeat it.

Instead, I tell him he should kiss me good night. He gets squeamish and does a lot of backpedaling, and I stand there impatiently wondering if he is a virgin. I can date a murderer, but I cannot date a virgin. No. Not again.

Eventually, he kisses me (briefly) and tells me he wants to hang out (do acid?) when he is back from Christmas. I nod and say I would like that, even though I'm not so sure. I wait for him to walk away before going into my apartment so that he does not know which unit I sleep in.

I crawl into my bed. I am so tired, but for the first time in a while, I am excited to wake up in the morning.

I take two melatonin and check Facebook. Nothing.

Part II

<u>**Monday, December 10, 2018**</u>

At work, I tell everyone about my date.

Alexis thinks that the arm-writing is endearing and says I should see him again. Megan makes me promise not to. He's too weird, she says. Even for me. I should date the other guy, the one who ran away from me at the party.

"He didn't even respond to my Facebook request."

"No one uses Facebook anymore; you should email him. Here, I'll help you draft something."

Cheyenne agrees. "You cannot date a man who talks about UFOs," she tells me when I call her on my way home from work.

The guy she's sleeping with, some political reporter, is on speaker. He agrees. "Do not see this boy again."

This is our first time talking, and I don't really like how narrow-minded he is.

"I'll let you guys get back to your date."

As I hang up, I get rear-ended.

The first time I got rear-ended was just over a year ago. I was still a production assistant, on my way to Gelson's to buy an expensive brand of Icelandic yogurt for the writers before lunch. I was at the red light at Franklin and Gower, singing along to The Cat Empire, when he hit me — he being an apologetic Israeli air-conditioner repairman who had been distracted by the news of a birth in his family. "I'm going to be an uncle! Can we please not go through my insurance?"

When I got back to work – lunch still magically on time – I told my boss that I was just hit by a car. He looked right at me and then walked away, taking his prosciutto and cheese sandwich into the writers' room: "How's the episode going?" That was the first time I realized I was disposable.

This time, I'm not upset. My muscles feel padded by a layer of general depression and sluggishness. I nod my head in acceptance (to myself? To God?) and pull off the freeway. Getting rear-ended in Los Angeles just seems inevitable, a matter of time.

———

Me:|Sorry I forgot to respond to you, I just got rear-ended.

Jesse: Oh no! Are you okay? Do you want to borrow my car while I'm away?

Me: You are not allowed to offer your car after a first date.

Jesse: Sorry.

Jesse: Do you want it?

———

My dad calls to check up about my accident, but I'm too tired from melatonin to really talk. He tells me that he is very proud of me. Both of my parents are very proud of me.

My mom warns me that bad things happen in threes.

———

<u>Tuesday, December 11, 2018</u>

I get to work on time and spend most of the morning attempting to email the Charlie Day doppelganger. Do I ask him out directly? Be more coy? Or do I pretend like I just want to know more about his work in tech? I work myself up into a state of mania and then send him something about getting drinks.

Around four, my boss gives me an assignment, Trey asks about our script and suddenly I have so much to do. I remind everyone I just got into a car accident; I can only handle so much.

When I get home, I do not need melatonin. I'm in bed and asleep by nine.

Wednesday, December 12, 2018

I'm getting sick. Probably from all the working out. My throat is sore, and I have no energy. I force myself to get out of bed and shower.

While brushing my teeth I listen to *The Daily*, the only news podcast I listen to. Every episode makes me cry, but it seems like required listening for white liberals, so I try to listen as much as I emotionally can.

A devastatingly humorless guy I went to college with is featured in this episode. He's a reporter at the *Times*, talking about the political nuances of the Senate. I get in my car and remind myself that it's fine to be mediocre. I remind myself of this three times because I still don't really believe it.

It's fine to be mediocre.

It's fine to be mediocre.

It's fine to be mediocre.

During lunch, I have a call with my agent. At least I think he is my agent. It's hard to tell because he has done absolutely nothing for me. On this call, he tells me that he will continue to do nothing for me.

"You're going to get your next job from your connections," he tells me. I think this is supposed to inspire me.

The first time I met my agent, he sat across from me and told me that I was going to make it, kid.

He's my age. He has huge hair.

Last December, he invited to me Gersh, a fancy office in Beverly Hills where he and two middle-aged men told me how great they thought my alien pilot was. "Do you have anything else?"

"I wrote something else about getting quarantined on a cruise ship indefinitely," I started, realizing halfway through that this is not the way to pitch an idea. "I hate cruise ships," I added, deadpan: "almost as much as I hate myself."

They loved that.

Today, he seems annoyed with me. He does not know what I'm writing (nothing), and I have been too busy working on a television show and gaining invaluable connections to call him.

"You could have called *me*," I point out. It is technically his job to call me. I was the one that set up this call. "I thought you were too busy working on a television show." His voice is an octave too high.

He is not impressed that when this show wraps, I will be paid to write Trey's feature since he won't get any money for that. Nor is he a fan of my *Weekend at Bernie*'s showrunner's assistant feature idea.[1]

He thinks there are too many scripts written about the entertainment industry and assistants. I should not write about an assistant, period. But I want to write a pilot about a female in the workplace. She is going to be an assistant. That's just how this world works. Aliens, he tells me, are also very 2016.

---

1. In which a showrunner dies of a heart attack and his assistant, a young woman, pretends that he is still alive so that she can finally gain respect in the industry through his dead (cis white male) corpse.

"But Tom Delonge is making a show about aliens now, can't you send my pilot to him?"

"Sure," he lies.

I hang up on him, frustrated, and send him a series of log lines for pilot ideas that I never intend to write.

———

Jesse: I want to take you out to dinner in Little Ethiopia

Me: I guess I'm free around nine.

Jesse: Great

Jesse: I'll pick you up?

Me: I can meet you there.

Jesse: you're coming from somewhere else?

Me: No.

Jesse: I really regret starting our conversation with an organ harvesting joke.

Me: Yeah.

Jesse: Can I start over?

Me: You can try.

Jesse: Hey, it's Jesse from Bumble. I'm not a murderer.

I drop my (dented) car off at home and call a fifteen-dollar Uber. While I wait for it, I tell my roommate that if I don't come home, it means that I've been murdered.

He's playing video games again: "Hey, when it's your time, it's your time."

It's a long Uber ride, so I call Cheyenne. She's alarmed. She understands why I may be intrigued by Jesse, but I also need to be careful.

"I'm being careful," I say. "I have mace."

Cheyenne thinks I do everything for the story.

"I do not. I'm just bored."

There is a difference here, however subtle.

———

Jesse is there when I arrive, hunched over a low table that looks too small for the both of us. The restaurant is colorful and empty, and the hunching looks uncomfortable, so I make him move to a normal table.

"Can I make a confession?" I tell him when we are reseated and still hunching.

"Okay."

"I have mace."

"Okay—"

"If I don't show up to work tomorrow, my coworkers will know it was you."

He does not seem to like this — but I cannot tell if it's because he doesn't like that I'm accusing him of murder, or if it's because I've undermined his plan to murder me.

"Can I make another confession?" I do not wait for him to answer. "I've started framing all of my thoughts as confessions because it adds an air of excitement that my life is otherwise missing."

I think that he'll appreciate this honesty, but he just looks down at his hands.

When the waitress comes, he orders a vegan plate for us to share and some honey wine.

"I'm sorry for ordering for you," he tells me. "But I know what is good here."

I — obviously — find this attractive, but I do not confess this to him. I like that he is uncomfortable.

The food comes out fast. The spongey bread covered in colorful vegetables looks like a paint palette. The food is incredible, and I like eating with my hands. It's more efficient like I've taken out the middleman.

"My fingers are probably dirty," I tell Jesse, "But I can't wash them because I don't want to leave my wine unattended with you — lest you poison me."

I'm virtue-signaling again: I'm Street smart, yes, but also very chill about germs.

Maybe it's because of the presence of the pepper spray, but Jesse says nothing about Satan on this date. He keeps introducing topics that are potentially alarming, but as he explains himself, they are not so weird after all. My mind is quieter tonight. I'm able to talk. To listen.

I complain to Jesse about my day – network TV and agencies. Inhaling some injera and wat, I tell him that if I had kids, I would encourage them to pursue money over passion because there is no real such thing as passion. He tells me that if he had kids, he would tell them to kill rich people. He starts going on about revolutions needing to be violent. I try to come up with a counterargument but fail.

"I don't have any money," I lie, "and if I die, what little money I do have will go to other rich people. You have no incentive to kill me. If anything, it will further concentrate wealth."

"I don't want to murder anyone. That was all hypothetical. I'm not a murderer, just a utilitarian."

"Are you good at poker?" I ask.

"Not really—"

"Do you think it's fine to lie to people if they're dumb enough to believe it?"

"No—"

"Have you ever hurt an animal?" I stare at him -- and check his face for any tells.

"Are you testing to see if I'm a sociopath?"

I am. "My old roommate had traits of psychopathy; some of them actually make you a good leader."

"I'm not a sociopath," he tells me.

"Well, you're at least on the spectrum."

"Will you stop saying that?"

He seems moderately annoyed.

"It's fine, I probably am, too." I try to subtly stretch out the elastic band of my tights. I overate.

I offer to pay this time, sincerely, and he shakes his head. He wanted to take me here, it is his treat. When the receipt comes, he tips and writes "Thank you" on the slip.

"Are you going to order another Uber?" he asks, tension in his voice.

"You can drive me."

He is relieved by this. He wants me to trust him.

I want me to trust him, too.

———

Jesse drives a blue hybrid. It's unremarkable save for a bright orange *Settlers of Catan* bumper sticker on the right lower corner. I get inside. His car is clean, almost empty. He's got hand sanitizer and a generic 7-11 brand antacid in the central console. I take one. It's not as good as regular Tums.

He starts to drive. My mace seems useless now that he's controlling a two-ton vehicle. Although his tank is almost empty, so we wouldn't get far.

"Do you need gas?"

"It's a hybrid, we're fine."

I try to talk to him, but I'm uneasy again, and I want to make sure he's taking me home.

"Did we just go South?"

"This road just veers. Do you want me to put your address in the GPS?"

I nod. He does, and I calm down.

We drive by a series of beautiful mansions in Hancock Park. Multi-million-dollar properties. My boss lives here.

"Would you kill my boss if I asked you to?"

He reminds me that he is not a killer, but in the small hypothetical world in which killing rich people would somehow redistribute wealth to the masses, he would support other people killing my boss. He does not want to do the actual killing.

This seems lazy.

"How do other girls respond to the kidney jokes on Bumble?"

"I don't know, I changed it just before we matched. It used to be a list of the animals I liked."

I wonder if I would have responded to that. "What's the list?"

"Cats, koalas, nudibranch sea slugs."

I look that last one up. The nudibranch is fluorescent-colored, translucent, and globular. This guy is on a permanent acid trip.

He pulls into my driveway and parks the car. I'm visibly nervous, even though it's clear he's not going to kill me now. He starts to tell me his opinions about Christmas lights (I asked him earlier, as a stall tactic when I thought he was driving the wrong way).

I have never been so disinterested in something someone has to say, and I sit there shaking while he finishes talking about how far we are from the sun. I start to open the passenger door and then stop.

"What's wrong?"

The sexual tension is unbearable, but he probably cannot feel it because he's divorced from his emotions.

"Normally, during a date, someone eventually kisses someone."

"The last girl I dated I met in Memphis. I don't know how to date in Los Angeles." As if this explains it.

I don't think making out in a car is unique to Los Angeles, but I tell him that's what he must do, not because I want him to, but because it's the rule.

"Okay. Can I kiss you?" He asks.

Obviously. I nod and tell him that he can.

He leans in, but he's not leaning in nearly enough, so I pull away. He apologizes, and I make him move his car so that it's not blocking the entire driveway. Then we kiss again. This time he is much better at it, and suddenly my tights are off. I think about inviting him up, but I still don't want him to know which apartment I live in, so we stay in the car. I never understood why people have sex in cars, and suddenly I get the appeal. We do not have sex (because I'm a lady!), but I stop worrying that he is a virgin.

Thursday, December 13, 2018

Dream Log: My Bubbie crashed my friend's birthday party – through the wall, à la the Kool-Aid Man – but instead of a pitcher, she's in a hospital bed holding an IV. I get in bed with her, and she repeats that it's all going to be okay. It's all going to be okay.

At lunch, all my male coworkers list movies that they think my female coworker Megan should watch. She is very open about wanting to watch more movies, but I still don't think she should have to listen to them, even if they're right about the Coen Brothers.

I'm annoyed because today everything is black and white; good or bad; condescending or not. After I tell the room that I didn't like *When Harry Met Sally*,[2] I realize I'm being extreme just to hear how it sounds, and I force myself to go on a walk. It's hot outside, and I sweat. I feel gross. I need to shower. I'm a disgusting human being.

My boss comes into the office and tells me he just went for a swim. He is trying to bond with me, I think because I used to swim a lot when I sprained my ankle. After work, I'd race over to the Rose Bowl Aquatics Center in Pasadena. Swimming was meditative. I had to turn my brain off to count the laps. Four slow, one sprint, three slow, one sprint, etc.

I stopped going when my underwater mp3 player broke and I got ringworm from the pool.

Today my boss swam at Equinox. He counted the laps, too. It was nice, he says, until he noticed a piece of hair floating in the hot tub.

"It was a rich person's hair, so it's probably clean," I tell him.

"It doesn't work like that." He shuts the door to his office. I have ruined things with him.

———

I want to see Jesse again, after work, but my female coworkers have planned a ladies' night, and I cannot ethically blow this off for a boy that I have just met on a dating app. We get quesadillas and manicures and talk about sexism in the workplace. Often the men zone out whenever the women pitch ideas. This is standard in the industry.

When I get home, I think about texting Jesse, but I am too tired.

———

2. I'm jealous that Harry and Sally have so long to figure out how they feel about each other. With climate change, I have at best ten years to fall in love with my friend.

<u>Friday, December 14, 2018</u>

My boss takes me on a walk around the lot to talk about my future. It's very stressful. "I have mace," I joke. He does not find this funny. Maybe I will stop telling people this. We pass by some cement stages and golf carts. I have worked for this man for two years, but I still have not figured out how to talk to him.

We end up sitting down at a picnic table outside of the cafeteria. I wish we had gone to the gazebo from the set of *Gilmore Girls* — it's more cinematic.

My boss tells me that if the show gets picked up for another season, I have a job and a promotion — he will let me write an episode for credit. But the show may never come back,[3] so I should probably look for other work.

I am a talented writer, he tells me, but sometimes I need to read the room and make fewer jokes. I have stopped making jokes, and people keep laughing at my serious pitches, but I do not say anything because the showrunner is always right.

When we walk back to the office, I feel disappointed. This is objectively the best way that the conversation could have gone — I have a job if I want it! — but it all seems a little beside the point now. Maybe because I feel like I deserved to write a script for credit a year ago. Maybe because the world is ending and spending another year in an airconditioned box thinking up ways that cops can shoot brown people seems like the wrong way to go out.

———

I cried the night I got agents. I cried and cried and cried. It felt wrong and hollow. I told myself it was just hormones.

———

Jesse: Did it ever snow where you're from?

---

3. Our ratings are bad, and our lead actor tried to quit publicly on social media.

Me: Why are you asking me this?

Jesse: Sorry. I'm just trying to be normal. Normal people talk about the weather, right?

I swoon. He is definitely going to kill me, but I'm glad he is playing the long game.

———

Saturday, December 15, 2018

At the gym, I notice that a guy I dated two years ago, Softboy, has friended me on Facebook. We dated around two years ago, right before Trump was elected when I had just been laid off from my terrible first job at a media startup.[4] He was half-Pakistani, very cute, very funny, very broke. We met on Hinge.

On our second date, he bought me dinner at a Korean place in a Chinatown mall (after I insisted he buy me food), and I could not eat because I was so nervous. When we went back to his place, he told me that he was looking for something casual.

"That's okay, I am too."

I only realized after it was too late that this was not true.

On the morning of the Women's March — we both had plans to go — I sat in his bed for hours explaining what oxytocin was.

"When you cuddle me, it makes me love you," I explained. "My hormones make me attached."

His eyes widened, blue and dumb: "It just makes me horny."

I hated myself so much. He hated himself, too. And we were missing the march! In a panic, he tried to drive me to Pershing Square, but the streets were blocked off, and it was too hard to park.

He told me he was moving in February. I tried to dump him first.

---

4. I was making "viral content." The place has since gone under.

———

I don't care about him anymore. I accept his request.

I lay down on the stretching mat, legs splayed in no particular pose, and pride myself on the fact that I've moved on.

———

I have a date tonight. Not with Jesse, but with someone else. I don't really want to go, but Jesse is still out of town. Plus, I have found it best to keep a couple of boys around to diffuse my neediness. If you are texting multiple boys, it's easier to forget when one does not text you back. I have been told that three is the perfect number of boys, but I have not made it there yet.

My date is running late, so I check Facebook and eat peanut butter out of the jar. I let myself think that I'm just browsing for alarmist news posts from Jade, but really, I know I'm looking for a message from Softboy -- maybe some sort of update that he has moved back to Los Angeles, or that he's been thinking about me a lot lately. My endorphins have worn off, so I can admit to myself that I care what he thinks.

I eat more peanut butter and scold myself for not having really moved on. It's been two years. I'm a loser.

I look at Softboy's profile. His friends are so funny. I wonder what my profile looks like to him. I scroll through it. I was so skinny in college. I was so skinny and so self-conscious and dumb. I'm curvier now. I'm curvy and self-conscious and slightly less dumb.

Why has Jesse not texted today?

———

I know, the moment I see my date, that this is not going to work out.

He's not unattractive. In fact, he looks just like his profile: round face, air of seriousness. But as I sit on the barstool next to him, sipping tequila soda with extra lime, I realize that I didn't inspect his profile close enough, because I'm not into it. He looks a bit like my dad.

Why am I here? Why am I going on dates when I just want to make out with a guy who's planning to kill me, maybe? But I'm here, and it's rude to leave right away, so I talk at this guy with the round face for a while.

He tells me a long story about seeing 50 Cent in Dodoma. Instead of listening to his story, I just think about how bad a person I am for not knowing where in Africa that is.

He has not had the forethought to write conversation topics on his arm, so we quickly run out of things to say and sit in silence. I don't want to know anything about him; he doesn't want to know anything about me.

We get another round because it's a Saturday night and we have nothing else to do.

———

Sunday, December 16, 2018

I'm worried about being alone with my thoughts today, so I text all my friends in the neighborhood.

Me: hey, do you want to go for a walk?

Me: hey, what's up?

Me: coffee?

Me: Hey, sorry I forgot to respond, what are you up to today?

I meet up with my friend Chris and his perfect boyfriend, and we hang out in his perfect Eastside Bungalow in Atwater with their perfect dog. Chris works in tech. His boyfriend is a documentary filmmaker. They treat me to a vegan Caesar salad. I tell Chris that he does not have to pay for me, but says he wants to. I'm his woman. I like this. I just want to be fed.

<u>Monday, December 17th, 2018</u>

At work, my mom sends me a video of a salamander she found while gardening and says it's her friend Shari.

Our family friend Shari has been sick in the hospital. My mom names animals after people she's lost. She saw a buck after her grandpa died, and even though she is not particularly spiritual, she still thinks it's him, coming to check on her.

I don't connect the two thoughts — Shari being sick, animals visiting as the dead — until my parents call me later in the day to tell me that Shari passed away. I'm driving home, maybe appropriately, maybe inappropriately, past the large cemetery on Forest Lawn Drive.

"Are you okay?" my mom asks me.

I am. I do not want to be sad right now, and I know it's calloused of me, but I don't want to have to deal with this. The world is ending, I have no space for more quotidian sadness.

But then my mom talks about the last time she saw Shari in the hospital, fighting for life, angry, scared to be alone. And I start to cry. Because where is she going? Why didn't we stay with her?

My dad is concerned: "Are you driving?"

I tell him it's okay: it's a rental car. And then we all laugh even though we're still crying.

At the gym, I cry on the spin bike. When I was five, whenever I cried people always gave me what I wanted. I know that crying is a privilege, and I feel bad about that, but I still cry because even with my privilege I cannot escape death.

I'm thinking all these things while a fit man in a tank top tells me to turn up my resistance so that we can pretend to ride up a hill. I try to disguise my tears as sweat. Maybe he'll think I'm just trying really hard.

I stay for yoga, and the instructor tells us all to give thanks for our bodies, and I do. Sometimes I just go through the motions, but today I mean it. I pull my legs in close and thank my body for existing.

———

Tuesday, December 18, 2018

After work and gym and peanut butter, I lie in bed. I cannot go to sleep. I look up at the ceiling and think about plastic. Only nine percent of plastic is actually recycled, and now the billions of tons that we have left to waste are coming for me. I see plastic in the roads, in the rivers, in piles, everywhere.

Shari's funeral is tomorrow. I will not be there.

Jesse: How are you?

Me: Stressed.

I feel better. Now that I have shared my anxiety, I can go to sleep.

———

Wednesday, December 18, 2019

At work, Megan catches me violently washing a bowl in the sink and asks if anything is wrong. I tell her everything is wrong, and that my family friend is dead. I'm fine though.

I go outside for some air and call my mom. She's cutting grapes for the funeral. Why the grapes need to be cut in half I will never understand.

"I'm sending you hugs," I tell her. Really, I'm sending me hugs. I want hugs.

Trey comes over and asks me if I've started reading *Drunk U.* He does not notice that I have an earbud in. I tell him that I'm on the phone with my mom because someone has died, and then I feel terrible for using this person that I care about as an excuse. I have not worked on the feature because I did not want to work on it. Because I am lazy. Because I am a bad person.

After a lap around the Warner Brothers lot, I calm down and join the writers' room.

We talk about the next season and come up with some cool stuff, but then my boss comes in with new marching orders, so none of it really matters anymore.

———

Thursday, December 19, 2019

I eat a leftover Banh Mi sandwich in the gym parking lot and then yell at my mom on the phone for no reason.

Me: Sorry, I love you. I just ate something spicy.

———

Tuesday, January 1, 2019

Things are calmer now.

I'm not sure what happened over my trip back home to Fairfield. I have a bad memory, so when I don't write things down, they blur. Maybe that is why I am keeping a diary, so that my life does not escape me.

I do know that I slept. A lot. And maybe it's because of the melatonin, but I feel like I'm living a dual life: awake me and dream me. Awake me had a relatively relaxing holiday at her childhood home in Northern California with her family. Dream me is writing for Ellen and is hunted by Nazis. Dream me has bangs!

———

Over break, I texted Jesse every day. I sent him pictures of my parents' dog (Rembrandt, an Australian Shepard), and he asked me annoyingly deep questions which I would ignore because I thought they were dumb.

Jesse: Do you fear death?

I do.

———

I cry on the plane back to Burbank. I cry because my brother doesn't want me to go with him to visit our sick grandfather in Michigan. He'd like to go alone. I cry because my grandfather is dying, and because my brother isn't going alone -- he's going with his fiancée, his new best friend.

I have one brother in Spain and one brother in D.C., and I know that this is natural and that we're all growing, but why do we have to grow apart?

I hide my face; I don't want to alarm anyone on Southwest.

Jesse is back, and even though I don't ask him to get me from the airport, I am thankful that I have at least one person waiting for me in LA.

———

Jesse: Do you still want to get dinner tonight?

Me: Yes but I am very sad.

Me: I may have to fetal position.

———

Jesse picks me up around seven, and we go to a Tunisian place. The food — lentils, vegetables, baklava — is delicious, but I'm wearing the tights with the control top again, so I can't eat that much. I lay down in the booth, pulling my knees up to my chest.

"I told you that I would have to fetal."

Jesse pays the bill.

"Do you want me to drive you home? Or do you want to come to my place?"

———

"I must be really bored to be doing this," I tell Jesse in the car, trying to hide my curiosity and excitement. He hears me but pretends not to understand that this is a dig at him.

He parks his car at the bank next to his apartment complex and pauses before we go inside.

"Dev might be meditating."

Dev is Jesse's roommate, an older Indian man. They share a one-bedroom apartment. Dev sleeps in the living room, and Jesse takes the room in the back for $700 a month.

"He does a lot of yoga," Jesse says. "He's in a cult."

When we enter, Dev is on a mat, doing some sort of meditation. An older woman is inside, washing dishes. "Hi Stella," Jesse says as he pulls me into his room and shuts the door.

"Who is Stella?" I whisper. "Do you think she thinks I'm a harlot?"

Jesse shakes his head.

"She's been around here a lot. I think she's an aspiring singer. She asked me about being in a band."

"She doesn't know how many dates we've been on, right?"

"You don't have to whisper."

———

Jesse's room is juvenile and bizarre. I'm immediately greeted by a stack of dirty dishes on his dresser, a soiled crock pot, and a stack of white ceramic bowls.

"You really cleaned up for me."

"I'm giving Dev his space in the kitchen."

Jesse has a single window and a small sliding closet, which he calls his library. He keeps his keyboard in his library, as well as a tiny bookshelf, a reading lamp, and a rug that I assume he curls up on while he reads. The back of the closet is lined with artwork made by his students.

He shows me one student comic strip that he is particularly proud of. In one panel, a dinosaur says something about invading a town, and the other dinosaur explains that there are people in there. In the final panel, the first dinosaur asks where the people will go.

"It's anti-humor," he explains.

Jesse really likes dinosaurs. He keeps figurines on his desk. He thinks that the triceratops is overrated and names all the other ones for me. I ask him if this is a *Big* situation. The writers discussed this at work. If he is really a 12-year-old in a 25-year-old's body, he has to tell me. I cannot have sex with him because it would be wrong. He laughs, but possibly only to evade the question.

There aren't many pictures in his room, but I find one of his dead cat (Copkiller) held by a woman with beautiful wavy blonde hair. Her back is to the camera, so I cannot see her face.

Jesse tells me that he spun around a globe and asked Copkiller where he wanted to go. His paw landed on the Grand Canyon, so he took him.

"I need to lay down."

I fetal on his bed. I'm ready to start making out. It's been a long day, and the picture of the blonde woman tells me that I can trust him. He cannot be so bad that a woman with beautiful hair won't go on a road trip with him. She doesn't seem worried about feline AIDS.

Jesse does not take the hint, so I tell him it's time to make out, and we start to kiss. He abruptly stops. He doesn't feel like making out sometimes, is that okay? It's not, but before I get a chance to tell him, we're kissing again.

We start to have sex, but the condom is too small, so I ask him to drive me home. He says that I do not have to leave right away, but I do.

"Did you mean that thing you said about not liking to kiss sometimes?"

"Did I say that?"

"You did."

"I don't remember. I just say things, sometimes."

———

<u>Thursday, January 3rd, 2019</u>

Megan has made a jab at Jesse. "You really know how to pick 'em," she tells me, while on the way to the body shop. My car is ready, so she's dropping me off. Megan is a good friend, and she's right: I'm picking them weird.

———

With this in mind, I finally agree to get drinks at Hyperion Public with a tall, basic guy I found on Hinge who has been harassing me over text for the last month.

Are we going to do this or what?

It is possible that he has bullied me into seeing him. I check him out in the booth before I sit down. He is handsome, but in an uneven way that makes me think he was kicked early in his youth. His vibe is princelike, douche.

I'm too exhausted to talk at him about the patriarchy or the end of the world, so we kind of sit for a while and I ask him if he's really a Buddhist like it says on his profile. He goes to a meditation in Silverlake once a month. I don't know if you can appropriate a religion, but if you can that's what he's doing.

My disinterest comes off as charming, and he keeps telling me how funny I am. He especially likes when I tell him I need to leave soon so that I can get ten hours of sleep, which is not a joke. I go to the bathroom to kill time, twice.

"Do you want to go out with me again?" he asks when I come back from my second bathroom trip.

"What? You can't ask this yet. You haven't even paid the bill!"

"I did while you were peeing."

"Oh."

"So? Do you?"

"I don't know. I need time to process the date."

"You know, you're really hard to read."

"It's hard for me to read me, too."

———

I see Jesse on Friday and then again on Saturday. On Sunday I take a lot of baths.

———

Monday, January 6, 2019

Dream Log: We know that the Big One is going to happen, so we break all of my mom's vases in advance.

———

<u>Wednesday, January 9th, 2019</u>

I'm up early and excited. I'm turning 26 today. It's my birthday! My day.

I do a yoga video to combat the aging. Leslie Fightmaster tells me that if my chakras are blocked, I'll have issues making decisions and enjoying sex. She does not tell me how to unblock my chakras, but I do some hip openers anyways, just in case.

Work is standard. We order vegan for lunch — my boss's suggestion, which is very nice of him — and I go to Starbucks to get my free birthday drink. It turns into a whole ordeal because my birthday drink coupon doesn't work on the lot and my reusable mug is leaking.

"Do you want a disposable cup to help catch the coffee from your reusable mug?" the barista asks, as I stare down at the hot brown liquid dripping onto my leg.

"I do not."

Around four, my boss dismisses us. As we all get up, Alexis clears her throat — a friendly reminder. We can't leave yet! It's my birthday, and we have to do my birthday surprise.

My boss is really into birthday surprises in the office. It's his way of saying thank you for working a sixty-hour week. They are not really surprises though, because we all know they are coming. Last year, when I was his personal assistant, my boss got me flowers and a big red panic button birthday cake.

"Did you get me these flowers?" I had asked, while perched at my desk, just in case the phone rang. They were a mix of roses, succulents, and something pink.

"No, I didn't. It must have been someone else in the office," he said, "What do you think? Do you like them?"

I didn't want to make him feel bad for not getting me flowers, so I told him they were sort of ugly.

He stormed off, offended. "It was me."

———

This year, there are no flowers. I know Sam bought me something because he texted me the night before asking me what I wanted and then told me what I wanted was too expensive.

"Maybe we can all go home?" I suggest, awkwardly, "I can eat my cake in the car?"

"Nonsense," my boss says. All the writers return to the table and do a very good job of pretending not to be annoyed that they have to stay late to celebrate with me. I grimace and wait for the cake. Except it's not even a cake.

Sam brings in birthday cake-flavored truffles from Milk Bar. A candle awkwardly shoved into one of them.

I want to cry.

The truffles are small and expensive, but they are not the same as a cake, and I'm disappointed. I know that I'm being silly. I'm twenty-six. I can buy my own fucking cake. And I hate myself a little, for being so entitled.

Some sort of awful repressed childhood trauma must have occurred at a birthday party because I am a monster. I am regressing. I try to hold back tears and be an adult at my place of employment, but it's hard because everyone is watching me.

"Are you having a party?" Trey asks.

"What are you doing to celebrate?" Patrick follows.

"Anything fun?" My boss.

"I am getting a fancy dinner at that new place in Los Feliz, Atrium?" I respond, my voice unsure.

I feel like a fraud. I don't like hip. I don't like fancy. I'm only getting dinner so that when people ask me what I'm doing on my birthday I have an answer.

The conversation turns to Patrick and his wedding, and I'm so relieved. I run to the kitchen and calm down.

"You can't run away from your own birthday," Trey jokes when he sees me deconstructing a birthday cake truffle over the sink. He is right, so I go back inside and ask Patrick if he is going to make all of his friends fly across the country for his bachelor party.

"That's a lot of jet fuel," I remark.

———

Fifteen minutes later, Megan walks with me to my car.

"We should have gotten you a real cake."

"Really? You think that?"

"Yeah. Those cake balls are really sad."

I want to hug her, but instead, I start to tear up. "My brothers emailed me happy birthday," I tell her. I don't want her to think that I'm tearing up over the lack of a cake. But also, it's true. Michael used to call. My college roommates used to text. The people who I celebrated with last year have left Los Angeles.

Everyone is disappointing me. I'm disappointing me.

"You can cry," Megan tells me.

I do. I cry in the car to the gym, on the treadmill, then back in my room. Normally I stop myself from crying for such selfish and utterly privileged reasons, but today, because it's my birthday, I allow myself to wallow.

I cry until my dinner plans, and then I stop crying because it turns out the hip restaurant is very nice, and my friends are paying.

———

I'm happy now. I'm with Chris and Casey. The overpriced cocktails are doing their job. I'm drunk.

Atrium is a strange place. It's half-greenhouse, half-movie set. The ceilings are high, and there are lots of trees, but all the furniture feels too light, almost fake.

We're picking at a variety of dishes: cauliflower shawarma, oyster mushrooms, brussels sprouts, beets. It's too much food, for sure, but our waiter – hot, disinterested – told us we needed to get at least three little plates per person. My friends don't seem to mind.

As I finish my second drink — something with thyme in it — Chris recounts the saga of our friendship. We both lived in the same dorm at Harvard, Dunster. College is a blur to me, but Chris remembers much more than I do. He was annoying back then; it was before he came out.

I vaguely remember him asking me to go for a run with him, and me artfully avoiding the question.

"It wasn't so artful," he tells me. "You used to panic and run away."

"I love you now," I tell him. "Now is what matters."

We pivot to boys. Casey tells me that I can't date Jesse because of the writing on his arm. I would not care what she thinks except for a few months ago when I was dating a magician, she told me to call it off. "You cannot fuck a magician," she told me. At the time I thought she was blindly obeying societal constructs, but I have since come to the realization that fucking a magician is something you can never take back.

But I like Jesse, so I make the case. "Sure, he wrote on his arm, but he is a good person. He volunteers. Back in December, he collected supplies for migrant refugees. Plus, he goes down on me."

"Do you like that?" Casey sips from her water.

"I don't really, but I heard somewhere that if men don't, they're selfish."

"Fine, you can see him," she concedes.

"Okay good, because we have plans tonight."

Casey and Chris both light up. Somehow this changes everything. "Tonight? What are we still doing here?"

I tell them that I am trying to value my time with friends over boys, but they really want me to get laid. They pay the check and drive me home. We are all excited for me.

———

Jesse comes over and hands me a card featuring a dog from *PAW Patrol*. "They didn't have many choices at the gas station," he tells me.

I open it. On the inside, he wrote: *Happy Birthday, I'm glad that you were born.*

I love it.

We have sex, but it's not great because of my chakras.

Afterward, I notice that his condom is a weird brand. He tells me that he got it from a sperm bank where he tried, unsuccessfully, to donate his sperm.

I thought Jesse's broke-ness was more of an accessory, a part of the socialist uniform. His brand. But he cannot take it off. He is making one thousand dollars a month. He is living on credit card debt. He cannot afford to live in Los Angeles.

And then he tells me. He's planning to move. At the end of the month, he won't be here.

In a way, I have known this for a while. But I tell myself I didn't really know. Jesse had mentioned it offhand, as a passing thought.

"Dev wants me out. I can't afford to live here. Maybe I should just leave LA?"

At the time I told him that he should move. I am always encouraging people to get out, because of the earthquakes. Also, I wanted Jesse to think I was chill, but what use is being chill if he won't be around to see it?

Maybe I thought that it wouldn't really happen, or that it would be a good thing. I told myself that this boy was not long-term. I would use him for unsatisfying sex and then find a normal guy who makes me laugh and who is weird in a socially acceptable way. I was not supposed to become attached.

I'm thinking so many things — all conflicting. I'm thinking that we should cut it off now. So that it hurts less when he does go. I'm thinking that we should stay together but just stop cuddling. No more oxytocin. On the other hand, maybe we should just lean into it and have the most passionate month of our lives. I think all these thoughts at once, but I can't tell Jesse any of them because they are all fighting to get out, and they all feel so useless anyway. There is nothing I can do to stop him from leaving me.

"I have thoughts, but I can't talk about them now," I say, face down on my pillow. I do not want him to see the tears.

"Okay."

"Can you stay over?"

"I parked in a spot that tows at 2 am."

I consider begging him to move his car and come back — it's my birthday after all — but for some reason, I believe that I get one beg, one trump card, and I would like to save it for something bigger.

Jesse tries to wait until I have fallen asleep to leave, but I'm still awake when he gets up. He's very loud locking the door behind him, so he would have woken me up anyway.

Part III

<u>Thursday, January 10, 2019</u>

I'm fragile today.

I call my mom on the way to work and tell her that I'm upset that my brothers didn't call me on my birthday.

"You cannot have it all," she tells me as I exit the 134 to Forest Lawn Drive.

I don't know what "all" refers to here — since I have neither a career nor a family — but I don't push too much because she tells me it's okay to be sad, and this is what I want to hear.

———

<u>Friday, January 11, 2019</u>

I wake up feeling better and wonder whether yesterday I was just going through alcohol withdrawal.

My brother Michael calls me drunk to apologize for not calling on my birthday. He feels bad. We were not supposed to be the kind of siblings who lose touch.

I forgive him, and he gives me a play-by-play of what's going on with his cat.

———

I have scheduled a date with a seemingly normal and attractive guy. Because Jesse is officially leaving, I want to get a jump start on moving on. It's not much of a jump start, though, because I have texted Jesse to meet me after he's done with his plans (D&D). Also, if he had been free to begin with, I would not be on this date.

We meet at the Dresden, and I worry that maybe the bartender (arm tattoos) is starting to recognize me because he winks at me when I order. If only he understood how walkable this bar is from my apartment.

My date is shy and reserved. He's Midwestern and has a wide face and curly blonde hair. We lob forgettable questions at one another, and I go to the bathroom to text my friends.

After a few hours and too many hints about it being my bedtime, ten on a Friday night, I tell him that I really need to go. He is not offended.

When Jesse comes over, he asks me who I was getting drinks with.

"A friend."

"Which one?"

"I don't want to talk about it."

I'm not good at this. Maybe I will stop trying to date multiple people.

———

Saturday, January 12, 2019

It's two o'clock in the afternoon. It's raining. I've been in bed for hours. Jesse is still here.

My parents are visiting for my birthday, staying at an Airbnb a mile away. I decide I will walk there. I feel weird seeing my parents after lying in bed all day with a boy, so I shower to cleanse myself. I don't want to be late because of Jesse, so I change my mind and tell them I'll drive.

Dad: there is no parking here.

I uber. There is plenty of parking.

———

My parents met in college, at the University of Michigan. My dad asked my mom out, but she wasn't interested. Then she changed her mind. As a romantic gesture, she made him a giant basket of blueberry muffins with a note: "The blueberry bandit has struck again." Except she didn't add sugar, so the muffins were inedible.

They moved to California in the 80s, because my dad got a job as a urologist. They could have stayed in Michigan, closer to family. I don't know why they came here.

Fairfield was very lonely. We lived on the outskirts of town, in the country, with two acres and a creek. The nature was beautiful though, like a Mary Oliver poem. We had blackberry bushes, oak trees, and a goat named Shadow.[1]

I was the only Jewish student at my school. I felt like a freak, and to top it off, my dad was constantly reminding me that everyone wanted to kill us. "Remember the Holocaust?" "The pogroms?" "The Inquisition?" Every historical figure was anti-Semitic. I couldn't even watch *Anastasia* because the Romanoffs were real, and they had killed all the Jews.

Adding to my worries, I alone was responsible for combating the diaspora, by popping out Semitic baby after Semitic baby. "If you don't marry someone who is Jewish," my dad told me once, "I will cut out my own heart."

He owned a scalpel. Who was I to doubt him?

When my brother got engaged (to a Jewish woman), he calmed down.

———

1. The goat has a strange story. For years I thought it had been someone's wedding gift that they couldn't keep, possibly even my dowry. But it turns out our possession of the goat was a product of divorce. Another doctor had bought the goat for one of his nurses, who he was also sleeping with. She couldn't legally keep the goat, so he kept it for her. When his wife found out, they split and moved. We had a big pen at the time, so that was that: they gave him to us.

My parents are happy to see me but tired. Their road trip from Fairfield to Los Angeles was about six hours. Rembrandt pees from excitement when he sees me. This is the energy I crave. We quickly lead him outdoors.

The Airbnb they're staying in is quaint and perfect, a little cottage with a big backyard and lights strewn across the fence. My dad estimates that it must be worth $1.2 million. He would buy it if he could.

In the living room, there is a large bookcase full of cookbooks, yoga guides, and photos. I pick up a wedding portrait. The bride is tall, blonde, and attractive. The groom is plain-looking, dressed sharp. I bet they tried Atrium. I bet they liked it.

We order in.

After dinner, I lay on my mom's stomach for an hour. My mom is sad. There has been a lot of death, not just Shari. I try to crawl back into her womb to cheer her up.

"You're right on my hip."

"Sorry."

To get me off her, my mom shows me a book about Hashimoto's Thyroiditis — a surprisingly common thyroid disorder that we both have.[2] The book claims that many of the things that I just assumed were part of my personality — depression, forgetfulness, anxiety, acid reflux — are in fact a result of my thyroid condition. And that many of my favorite things — gluten, dairy, alcohol, coffee, chocolate, sugar — make my symptoms worse.

If my thyroid were functioning, would I not be like this? So sad? Would I be a normal person? Would I be like Sam? Happy? On the other hand, my aloofness is part of my charm.

---

2. Senior year of high school a child endocrinologist told me that if my thyroid was the mailman, and my hormones were the mail, then I have dogs in my body that are attacking my thyroid and making it hard for it to deliver the post. I do not remember what the dogs represent, but at the time I was acing anatomy and physiology and could have handled scientific terms.

"Why didn't you tell me that my thyroid did this to me?" I ask my mom.

"I didn't know."

———

Sunday, January 13, 2019

My mom's doctor told her to start doing yoga for her arm strength, so I take her to a class at a nearby dance studio with an instructor, Tara, that I know from my gym. Tara exudes wisdom. She's a former lawyer, a former actress, probably in her late sixties, small, Black, powerful, and lately, sad. She has just been evicted from the Frogtown apartment where she lived for twenty years to make room for a luxury condo. Her mom, in Brooklyn, is sick.

We are almost late, and the other women with mats already set up are not excited to see us. They are cold — both in personality and body temperature — and they bark at me for leaving the door open. I didn't know it was mine to shut!

My mom is not good at yoga. I try to get her to modify, but she is stubborn, and during downward dog, she bursts into a fit of laughter because she can barely hold herself up. I know I should be laughing with her, bonding, because that is what would happen in a Nancy Meyers movie. But I don't. The cold women are there, and even though they are in front of us, I can feel their third eyes glaring at me.

Afterward, Tara tells me that I'm lucky to have a mom who can do things with me.

———

Monday, January 14, 2019

My parents leave town, and I go to work. I wonder why I am living here.

I have nothing to do in the office. I should be writing, but it seems easier to spend money, so I buy all the expensive things I have been putting off: plane tickets, a bachelorette dress for my brother's wedding.

When this job is over, I will have nowhere I need to be again. I can go anywhere. I can do anything. Move. Travel. Start over. I'm overwhelmed with opportunity, and as a result, I'm paralyzed. I call my parents. I want to complain about how I have no direction, but it turns out that they are stuck on the Grapevine – the portion of Interstate 5 that weaves through the mountains.

"We haven't moved in three hours," my dad tells me. He sounds chipper; it takes me a moment to register what he's saying.

"What?"

My mom explains that the freeway has been shut down because it started to snow. They have no idea what is going on.

"Your mother peed in a dog dish!" Again, why does he sound upbeat?

It's snowing and they're low on gas.

I hang up and call Caltrans, panicked. They do not know when the freeway will reopen, but the dispatcher assures me that my parents will not starve to death.

"There is a dog in the car," I say, just in case this woman is the type of person who likes dogs more than people. "I don't want them to have to eat the dog."

"The dog will be fine."

I hang up and look at Twitter. A lot of people are stuck on the highway, and a lot of tweets are about global warming. This was a bad idea.

I studied environmental science in college. It was my minor. At first, I studied government, but after a "Military Interventions Seminar," which caused reoccurring nightmares about nuclear winter,[3] I switched to a major less upsetting: environmental science.

Or so I thought.

Climate change didn't feel immediate back then. Perhaps because my curriculum was partially influenced by the Koch Brothers. [4] I didn't question it at the time, but my geology class about "Earth Resources and the Environment" was taught by a former petroleum engineer.

I learned in my lab how to use seismic imaging to find oil. We took a three-day field trip to Pennsylvania – to open pit coal mines and to a fracking site (Chesapeake Energy). A host at the site fed us dry sandwiches, gave us plastic water bottles, and told us how safe hydraulic fracturing was. "We have so many government regulations!" As if they were the victims in this.

I did not fully believe him, but I still walked out of that class spewing a line that I would later hear from the gas company itself: "Sure, natural gas is not perfect, but it's way cleaner than coal, and it is a great short-term solution as we transition to clean energy."

This was Spring 2013. Many of my classmates went on to work in Canadian oil.

It wasn't until this October when Casey texted me about the United Nations' IPCC report, the scary one, the one that said we only had twelve years to change things, that I realized just how wrong I was.

Did you read this? We are all going to die!

---

3. One particularly problematic nightmare involved me and all of my college roommates. The nuke was about to drop, and we had to get to Sigma Alpha Epsilon, the only shelter on campus.

4. Harvard has received millions of dollars from the Koch brothers, has not divested its billion-dollar endowment from fossil fuel companies, and profits (tax-free) from natural gas reserves in Martin County, Kentucky where water is undrinkable.

I looked around at my coworkers — smart people that I had wanted to impress, wanted to be, just moments ago. "Have you seen this report?" I asked. Megan shrugged. Trey smirked. Patrick sighed. "What can you do?" And they all went back to trying to make the car chase in Act Five less derivative.

"What if we chased the bad guys up a parking structure... but it's the wrong one?"

I excused myself and had a panic attack in the bathroom.

Why did I think we had more time?

————

I stress-eat another bowl of grapes. I don't remember eating the first bowl, but the bag is nearly empty.

"Has anyone else been eating grapes?" I ask the office. No writers are in today, so it's pretty much empty. At the far end of the hallway, Alexis shakes her head. So, it was me who ate the grapes, after all. I feel insane.

I try to distract myself by offering to help Sam clean the whiteboards in the conference room. After thirty seconds I give up. I can't stop thinking about the Donner Party. At what point did they eat the dog?

Over five hours later, California Highway Patrol starts releasing cars, six at a time. My parents are moving, albeit in the wrong direction. They'll have to drive back down to Los Angeles and then take the 101 back up. My parents seem to have accepted this fate, but I'm anxious. It will be another eight hours in the car.

I wonder if worrying about your parents makes you an adult.

I text Jesse.

Will you come over?

Jesse does not respond. I have become too needy. Maybe I will buy a body pillow.

I go to the gym and once I start running, I feel better. About everything. My parents, climate change, Jesse. It's only once I decide that I don't need to see him that he finally responds to tell me he's free.

He doesn't stay late because he has work, and I'm annoyed. I try to play it off as sleepiness. When he leaves, I vow to ignore him for a day so that I seem more chill. I want him to text me first. Miss me.

————

Tuesday, January 15, 2019

Me: How's it going? How's the teachers' strike?

Jesse: It's fine, I was able to get to work without crossing a picket line.

————

Wednesday, January 16, 2019

Up early, I walk to the library to return a book I never got around to reading (*Kitchen Confidential*, by Anthony Bourdain). It's nice out. The soft rain is creating an eerie mist.

Jesse's apartment is right across the street from the library. I tell myself I'm not looking for him, but I find myself scanning his street, his door. It's 8 am, and he should probably move his car out of the Bank of America parking lot. Almost as if willed, I spot him on Franklin getting out of his car.

He cannot see me like this. I'm wearing unflattering shorts and an oversized orange sweater and listening to an RFK conspiracy podcast. I feel crazy. He'll think I'm stalking him. I'm not! He just happens to live by the local library which I just happen to use! I try to act normal; how do you act normal when the man who actually assassinated Robert Kennedy is still out there?

I duck my head under my umbrella and speed-walk away.

When I get to work, Megan and Alexis tell me that I cannot text Jesse to tell him that I saw him parking his car and running away. I could have said "hi" to him at the time but texting him later in the day is the creepiest of all the permutations.

I ignore them.

Me: I saw you during my walk to the library but then I hid from you because I didn't want you to think that I was stalking you.

Jesse: I feel so violated!

I show everyone the text. "See, it was fine to text him, he's a good sport."

Megan tells me that he is perfect for me. Alexis is annoyed: she's been saying this the whole time!

My heart pangs because now that other people have said it, I can agree.

———

Despite my unintentional stalking, Jesse wants to see me, so he invites me to work with him at a café. I know that by "work" he means apply to jobs in Austin — where he has decided to move — but I agree to go with him anyways. Maybe I can sabotage his job applications.

But first, I have a Greenpeace volunteer video call. I'm not active in Greenpeace, but I used to donate monthly (they cornered me outside Whole Foods and asked me if I like trees), and I must have signed a lot of petitions because they have my number and texted me an invitation to a Los Angeles Volunteers call.

I assume that there will be hundreds of volunteers (this is LA, after all, don't we all like trees?) and that it will be the kind of call where I can put my computer on speaker and then walk out of the room and make popcorn and come back and feel good about doing my part. But this call is not like that. It's intimate. There are only eighteen of us, and we all have to go around and share our names, preferred gender pronouns, and what inspired us today.

"Joelle, she, her, hers, and um... this call? You guys are inspiring."

I'm an idiot.

Someone talks about their plastic campaign. I ask early on how I can get involved, and the facilitator tells me that we'll get to that later.

What am I even doing here? They must have texted me by mistake. Everyone else seems to know what they're doing. Everyone else is inspired by life. I do not belong here. I am the problem, not the solution. I want to hang up, but I don't, because they will surely notice the attendance dropping to seventeen. Eventually, they tell me that they'll be going to Trader Joe's with thousands of petitions next week to demand that the store go plastic free. This is how I can get involved.

I make a mental note to go to the protest so that my presence on the call will not be a total waste.

————

Jesse picks me up, and after a lap around the neighborhood, we end up at the Starbucks three blocks away from my apartment. I don't want Jesse using plastic in front of me today, so I buy him a ceramic mug when he orders a hot chocolate. He's happy to get new dishware, but he points out that it's a little dirty.

"Can you rinse it out?" I ask the barista.

He nods, "Sure."

"What are you doing?" Jesse asks me. "Have you ever worked in food service before?"

"I have. I was a barista in college." I do not tell him it was four hours a week at the English Department café, because we both know that doesn't really count.

"Why make their work more difficult?"

I'm angry. I was doing this for him. He said the mug was dirty, and who am I not to act on that? Also, he's being sexist. I'm so tired of white men who think they are radical putting down women for not being radical in the same way. I can't make a reasonable request without being told I'm demanding.

Jesse apologizes. He did not mean most of what I'm accusing him of. And I accept his apology because I never really thought he did either. Maybe I'm overcompensating for never really having worked in food service.

It's almost nine PM. Starbucks is empty.

When we sit down, I ask him if he regrets inviting me. He shakes his head.

"I think I'm just upset that you're applying for jobs in front of me." This is a lie. I am upset about both things equally, but one seems more petty.

"Do you want me to pretend that I'm not?"

"Yes."

"Okay. I'm not applying for jobs."

He pulls out his laptop. His hair is greasy under his purple beanie. I ask when he is leaving Los Angeles, and he tells me the first weekend of February.

"I'll be unemployed then," I say.

"Do you want to go with me?"

I nod. "I would."

I'm calmer after that. I drink his hot chocolate and work on my pilot, "Dad Planet," which is not really about anything yet, but I like the idea of a young girl running away with a sex robot only to wind up on a planet full of men. Jesse came up with the title and said if I wrote it, I could win his respect.

I show him the teaser, and he loves it. I'm good at writing the first five pages, but I have no idea where it's going. Where is anything going?

"Why don't we finish *Star Wars* to inspire you?" he suggests.

———

It is late and he is holding me. He is saying a lot of sincere things that I didn't realize I needed to hear.

His moving has nothing to do with me. He is not moving because I'm not enough for him. I am enough for him. If he was not moving, this would have turned into something real for him.

"Would this have turned into something real for you?"

I nod, but I do not tell him that it already has.

When he asks me if I'm lonely, I do not answer, because I'm lonely even with him next to me, and I do not want to cry in front of him. I do not want him to pity me. He must pity me because I never finish when we have sex.

I feel broken. He tells me that I'm not broken. I roll onto my stomach and mumble into my pillow. It's probably my thyroid. When he leaves around one, I do not ask him to stay.

———

<u>Thursday, January 17, 2019</u>

It's raining hard this morning, and I'm still tired, so I put on Leslie Fightmaster to get some energy. The video is entitled, "Leslie's favorite flow." It starts out slow, but then all of a sudden she is doing handstands. I cannot keep up. Leslie has tricked me. I can trust no one.

I get to work late. In an attempt to accomplish something, I lock myself in an empty office and stare at five different drafts of scripts — all teasers.

Around noon I give up and go home.

———

Drew, my friend from college, is visiting from New York. Drew works at Google. Or at least he did because they shut down his department but are paying him for the next three months to not work and to think about what he wants to do with his life. I am jealous, but I remind myself that I will soon be on California Unemployment Insurance.

He gives me a big bear hug when I see him. He was in the Lampoon with me, in fact, we were hazed[5] together, which makes for quick bonding. He was one of the nice boys. But to be fair, when you remove them from the collective, most of them are nice.

"Where do you want to go for dinner?" I ask. I wish I had food in my house so that I could feed him.

"I don't care, I'm just happy to see you!"

In college, Drew and I always joked about getting married. Senior year for Christmas, I got on one knee with a Ring Pop and proposed. I even registered our fake wedding at Bloomingdales.[6]

He thought it was so funny that he wanted to get married as a prank at City Hall, even though he had a boyfriend at the time. I said no.

———

We walk to get Thai food. On the way back I get annoyed with Drew for not thinking everyone should eat less meat for environmental reasons.

He loves meat. I tell him that I love life. I just want to make it to forty. I don't understand how people would rather have the world end early than give up hamburgers.

He tells me this is a false dichotomy, and that we should go after the oil and gas companies first. I don't disagree, but I can't go after the oil and gas companies. All I can do is eat less meat and yell at my friends.

———

---

5. Or I suppose, according to the Massachusetts hazing law I signed, we were "not hazed" together.

6. I asked for three knife sets and a vacuum.

<u>Friday, January 18, 2019</u>

When I wake up, I pretend to be alarmed that I slept ten hours. "This was not my plan!" I tell Drew. "I never sleep this much!" He believes me.

"Also, sorry my bathroom is a mess."

Since the office is empty again, I bring Drew to work so that he can see that even though I'm not paid as well as employees at Google, I'm well-fed.

I walk him through our kitchen. We have two fridges — one for drinks, one for fruit and Icelandic yogurt — and three cabinets full of all the snacks you could think of — cereal, oatmeal, cookies, crackers, chips, chocolates, nuts, protein bars, almond butter, candy.

"You want coffee? Matcha? Le Croix? Do you have an Egg McMuffin maker at Google?"

"We don't."

Lunch comes later than usual because Trey has asked Sam to bring his lunch order directly to his house. He is not coming in today but still wants free food. I lock eyes with Alexis. We both think this is not fair, but we can't say anything because Trey might get us all jobs one day.

Instead, we talk about boys and careers, even though I feel like mine is ending. Alexis is starting a new job next week and apparently pitching a feature to Lifetime. Sam is going to try to work on another show.

We raid the kitchen and leave the office with bags of food. In traffic, Drew pulls out his laptop and looks up all the discounts he can get in Los Angeles for being a Google employee. He's talking about ten percent off a trip to the Galapagos when I pull into my driveway. I don't think anyone should be traveling there other than scientists — tourism is bad for biodiversity — but I don't tell him this.

———

I need to work out for my mental health, and Drew does not want to come with me, so I take my car and head to the gym. Traffic is especially congested, so it takes me twenty minutes to go the two miles to my gym in Atwater Village. I don't mind. I call my parents.

My mom is excited to hear that Drew is thinking about moving to Los Angeles.

"Is he moving there so that he can date you?"

"He's gay, Mom."

"Why don't the good ones like you?!"

———

Drew and I go to Silver Lake to meet up with his friend at some sort of party for funny people. The bar is too expensive for comedians and too crowded to hear what people are saying — jokes, presumably.

I see a guy I don't like from college, and he tells me what he's been up to — comedy, lots of comedy. I pretend to be surprised, even though he sends me a weekly email asking me to come to his shows. I think I hate him. I also wonder if I'm jealous. I don't think it's right that he gets to be so confident about himself when he's only marginally funnier than I am.

———

I did some stand-up in college during my senior year. My jokes were, for the most part, self-deprecating. It was fun, then, performing in the Science Center, in lecture halls mostly full of freshmen eager to support their roommates and friends.

Los Angeles was different. The open mics were depressing, the audience was mostly other comedians waiting to go up. No one stayed after they went on, so if you went up last, there'd be no one left to see you. I tried out a couple in the basement of a wine store in Atwater Village.

The night I officially retired, I was last on the list and performing after "Krystal the Pistol." She seemed very drunk and very sad, tearing herself apart on stage. "I'm Krystal the Pistol!" I remember her shouting into the mic, voice frayed at the ends. "I want to abort myself!"

I had to follow her. I stood on the "stage" – it was more of a clearing in front of some chairs – and looked out at the audience which consisted of my roommate and one stranger from Texas.

I did not want to do this. I did not want to brutalize myself to be heard.

———

Years later, when I told a cute boy about the situation, he told me that he knew Krystal. "She's actually doing really well."

———

I'm in the bathroom now. Inside, I breathe in and out. There's a scented candle in the corner, and it's spacious. I can spin around with my arms open, so I do. I am calm.

I sit on the toilet and text Jesse.

Jesse: How is your friend?

Me: I'm hiding in a bathroom.

I want Jesse to come out and save me from this bar, from the comedians. The idea of asking him to do so does not cross my mind. I have gotten so used to hinting and waiting. The guy will come save me if I hint and wait and sit in the bathroom enough.

I leave the bathroom and resolve to have a good time while I wait to be saved. There is a cute boy in the group of comedians. It seems like he is just friends with a comedian and not actually trying to be one, so I talk to him. I cannot date a comedian, but I forget my reasoning why.

We are both from the Greater Sacramento Area, so I ask him if he's seen *Lady Bird*. He leans over me and shakes his head, no. He can't see the movie because he's single. He continues to tell me that he was dating a girl for eight years, but they broke up because he wanted to have kids and raise them outside Los Angeles, and she didn't want to ever leave the city. And he can't see a movie unless he has a girl to discuss it with afterward.

So no, he hasn't seen *Lady Bird*, because he had no woman to explain the movie to.

I call an Uber.

———

Me: Are you awake?

Jesse: Yes.

Me: Hypothetically, if I paid your uber, would you come over?

Jesse: It's kind of too late. I'm too tired.

Me: I didn't invite you! It was hypothetical!

Jesse: I respect you

Jesse: You are independent

Jesse: You shouldn't even want my company

———

I vow that Jesse is dead to me, and then I apologize to Drew because he has never seen me like this.

He reminds me that he has seen me like this. Multiple times.[7]

———

7. Two years ago, when I was sad about Softboy, and four years ago, when he lived in San Francisco, and I hooked up with his roommate.

Sunday, January 20, 2019

Drew is up early. He's going to a friend's house to film a podcast about staying positive. He's going to talk about dinner parties and dogs.

I tell him I'll work out while he's gone, but instead, I clean. I wash my sheets and his sheets, and I wash the disgusting mat on the floor of my bathroom, which I have not cleaned for over a year.

I try to scrub the toilet with a toothbrush, but I don't have bleach, so it's kind of useless, and I'm not sure why I'm using one of my nicer toothbrushes.

I feel disgusting. Why was I so sad last night? Why was I so needy? Now I have burdened other people with my irrational emotions.

By the time Drew gets back, I have gone through my entire dresser and set aside a large bag to donate to Goodwill. I feel better about where I'm living, if not how I'm living.

I'm embarrassed about last night, so Drew reads my texts to Jesse and tells me that it's not so bad.

"You didn't respond to a lot of what Jesse said."

"That was intentional. I was trying to convey deep pain."

"I'm not sure that reads."

None of this matters to Drew, anyway. He knows I have a date tonight with a cute Harvard Law School grad, and after reviewing his Hinge profile, he's rooting for this guy. I think the lawyer will be a waste of time — he was boring over text — but I do agree he's cute, and maybe I should date someone who is not moving away forever.

Drew leaves. So, I go to a park in Sherman Oaks to clean up garbage with Greenpeace. (One of the volunteer events mentioned on the call.)

The park is massive. There are baseball diamonds, playgrounds, an archery center, and I would not be surprised if I came across a zoo. But my directions to the meeting spot were vague, and I cannot find Greenpeace. I circle around for five minutes and think about giving up. I tried to be a good person; that is what counts.

I'm about to turn around when I spot a girl in with a bunch of gloves and a clipboard.

She's young, with French braids and a baby face. A kid. They all are. It turns out Greenpeace is teaming up with a Girl Scout working on her Gold Award. Everyone here is in high school.

I feel out of place and don't know what to say. I stand there awkwardly as a fourteen-year-old hands me a garbage bag and gloves. "We cleaned out this river a couple of months ago," she tells me, "But it's all gross again."

———

I spend the next three hours picking garbage out of a ravine.

I pull out a lot of wet clothing, all abandoned and covered in worms. I wonder whose clothing it is: size 34 jeans, a sports bra, a flannel.

I also pick up plastic bags and plastic bag fragments. I find a sad sense of irony in the fact that we are filling big plastic bags with smaller plastic bags. We are using so many garbage bags that I wonder if it would just make more sense to pile the garbage in a neat corner of the river and designate it as a new dump.

I don't say this aloud, of course. I don't say much of anything. I just pick in silence. I pick around a giant tree. It's so big that I climb on top of it to collect the garbage. As I pull out a pair of earplugs entangled in a branch I whisper into the bark: "Sorry I let this happen."

One kid does talk to me, a chubby girl with braids. "Are you in high school?"

"Oh, I actually graduated college. I work on a TV show about cops."

"Wow, that's so cool."

In high school, I wanted to grow up to be a political satirist or a journalist. I wrote a lot of op-eds in my high school newspaper about food waste, sweatshops, and fascist immigration laws. I was very idealistic and condescending.

Junior year, I held a month-long boycott of sweatshop labor. I handed out orange strings to wear as bracelets to people participating. A girl on my tennis team, Billy, told me that it was stupid and useless. Besides, I was a hypocrite. She pointed at my Nikes. "These are old," I told her. "The boycott is just to raise awareness."

By the time I got to college, I just wanted to be liked.

I tell the high schooler that I used to be a Girl Scout, too. "I quit, though, in middle school, because I didn't think it was cool."

————

I walk into the Dresden for my date with the lawyer. I'm surprised I didn't cancel, given how many bathrooms I've cried in and how much garbage I picked up today. I am still so hungover that even the thought of drinking makes me gag. I tell myself I'm here for Drew. Also, Jesse won't see me until Monday (tomorrow). I don't have to drink. I can get juice.

The bar is empty tonight, so my date, Spencer, is easy to spot. He is sitting in the center of the bar surrounded by empty round tables. I think this is a weird choice. I would have sat off to one side.

Spencer is cute. He's a little short, which I normally do not mind, but I feel huge today because of my body dysmorphia. Slightly too large, everywhere.

He stands up to hug me and then sits back down and dives immediately into small talk. He's a fast talker. Animated. His questions come out in bursts. "I worked all day today, what did you do?" He sits there, like a squirrel, waiting for me to feed him a breadcrumb.

I swivel in my chair and tell him how I cleaned up a bunch of garbage in a ravine.

He opens his eyes wide and tells me that's very attractive.

"I'm an environmentalist," he tells me.

"Do you do environmental law?"

"No, I work in legal malpractice. But I plan on buying a Tesla."

We talk, and I'm pleasantly surprised. There are no lags in conversation, and he is much more interesting than the app version of him who had very little to say.

Even though I'm feeling huge, and I promised myself I wouldn't drink, I find myself agreeing to go with him for a second drink at the overpriced French place up the street. At a small table, surrounded by couples sharing carafes, and he tells me about his friend who worked for Lindsey Graham.

"He's the senator of South Carolina," he clarifies.

"I know who Lindsey Graham is," I lie.

We talk more. I find myself bringing up my bat mitzvah multiple times. I'm coming off as too Jewish, I think. Maybe he is Jewish?

"Are you Jewish?"

He shakes his head. "Basically." He's Persian. His parents fled Iran during the revolution. "I've had a very comfortable life, though."

"Yeah, me too."

———

Around eleven, he panics because he needs to get to work tomorrow. He calls an Uber, but not before giving me a string of compliments. "Let's do this again?"

I nod my head. "I had a good time." I think that I mean it.

———

<u>Monday, January 21, 2019</u>

Dream log: TSA Agents search my carry-on. I thank them, one by one, for working during the government shutdown without pay.

———

I have plans to take shrooms today with Jesse. I made the plans when I thought we would get MLK Day off, but it turns out only Alexis has been formally told that she could stay home.[8]

I don't get vacation days, and I'm not great at skipping work, so instead of just one excuse I end up giving my coworkers three:

1. I'm sick (to be fair, my throat does hurt from all the drinking).

2. I'm being productive at home (I have no work to do so it's unclear even to me what I mean by this).

3. It's MLK Day, and we should all get the day off.

I feel bad about that last one — using MLK to skip work and do drugs — so I read up on civil rights before Jesse comes and vow not to be a passive white woman.

When Jesse arrives around one, I think about telling him how disappointed I am with him for not seeing me over the weekend.

"Do you want lentil soup?" I offer instead.

"I'm good. You're not supposed to eat before doing shrooms."

A pang of rejection flows through me — I am annoyed that he doesn't need food the way I need food.

He puts his backpack on my table and pulls out the shrooms in two Ziplock bags. The mushrooms are big and twisted and kind of beautiful — grayer than I would have

---

8. For some reason my boss only gives Black people the day off.

expected, like the branches of a burnt tree. I only want to eat half of an eighth, I tell him. He tells me I should eat the entire bag.

"Do you trust me?"

He's being emotionally manipulative, and I don't know why he's making me weigh my trust for him against the Reddit thread I read about taking shrooms with a cold. I eat the entire bag anyways, mostly because I like the way they taste.

I want to go to a park and look at nature because that's what I've been told to do on shrooms, but Jesse thinks it's too windy. We lay on my bed for a while and listen to the music he worked on instead of hanging out with me. The music is upbeat, alternative, and funky, his voice-high pitched and whiney. It's good.

"I only want to do things that make me like you less," I tell him, turning off his music.

He nods and pulls out his favorite comic book.[9] It's not very funny or interesting. It's just about a witch driving alone in the car. We skip to the end.

When I mention his drive to Austin, he says he is excited to do it alone. He does not even remember inviting me.

I do like him less now.

At this point he asks for a tarot card reading, so we sit on the floor, and I pull out the deck my brother bought me years ago when he went to New Orleans.

Jesse's critical of the way I shuffle the cards. "You've left two out."

"How do you know that wasn't meant to be?" I point out to the light streaming through my blinds. I explain it's the power, and I'm just a cipher, and then I get too distracted by the color of the cards to finish the reading. They're so bright and blue.

I'm definitely high now.

Why didn't Jesse take me to the park? I am feeling this way about laminated paper when I could be feeling this way about the trees or the sky.

---

9. Megahex by Simon Hanselmann.

He's uncomfortable now, so he wants to move back to my bed. I think I'm being profound, so I tell him we're not compatible because he prefers the bed and I prefer the ground; I want to be with him all the time, and sometimes he needs to be alone.

I feel all-knowing, confident, alert. I am in control, and I trust myself. This is not what I expected from shrooms. I look down at my foot. It's hideous, small, and misshapen, pulsating: smaller, larger. I'm thinking how ugly my foot is when suddenly I see all the little red blood cells and capillaries moving through it, the blood circulating, carrying oxygen and nutrients from my heart to the tips of my toes. I'm overcome all at once with a warmth, a hug from the inside out.

My blood is working so hard, so hard, and my foot is not ugly, because it's home to the thousands of tiny little blood cells. I don't just know this: I experience this, perhaps for the first time in my life.

Jesse is worried now. "Why are you crying?"

I don't want to share my knowledge because I'm so wise now, and I don't need him — his face looks like a troll — but he is so concerned because I'm crying so hard. I tell him they're tears of understanding because I'm not alone. I will never be alone. I will always have my blood.

It's a shame we all hate our bodies when our blood is working so hard.

I laugh at myself. I am being so cliché. I sound like the type of white woman who is vegan and does yoga. I suppose I am that woman.

I join him on the bed now because I'm exhausted from all my profundity. I want it to stop. But when I close my eyes, I still see shapes and movements — reds, oranges, yellows, dancing behind my eyelids. I'm briefly alarmed. "How much longer will this last?"

"A while."

Jesse tries to distract me. He pulls a book from my nightstand. Another. I shake my head. I do not want to read. He dances for me.

He looks stupid. I do not like him so much now that I have myself to like.

"I only ever dance for you," he tells me.

"I saw you dance on Instagram for Jeff."

He corrects: "I only ever dance for you and Jeff."

He stops dancing and pulls out my laptop. He wants to read my diary. I'm annoyed, not because I don't want him to read it, but because I wanted a proper distraction from my thoughts, and my diary is hardly that.

He doesn't stop though, and I must have given him my password because he opens the Word document and scrolls. I'm worried that he's not even reading my words — that he's just tripping on how the blurred document looks when you move through it fast, cool and infinite. But then he stops. He reads aloud. I listen.

He's reading about the night we met.

The words are strange and unfamiliar. I think he must have accidentally opened someone else's work because I don't remember writing all of this about him. I have written so much about him.

I don't want him to think he is the only thing that matters in my life but laying there watching the reflection of my words scroll through his eyes, I think that maybe he is. But also, I have never been this high. It could all be a hallucination.

He pauses when he reads about how he wrote "thank you" on the bill at the Ethiopian restaurant.

"I got this idea from someone else," he says. He looks up at me. "If you publish this, she deserves the credit."

"I'm not going to publish it. Besides, it's my diary. It's my perspective."

But then he's done reading, and suddenly he's pulling out his phone and calling that "someone else" and telling her that I wrote about her "thank you" in my diary and gave him the credit.

It's the girl from the photo. The girl with the great hair, holding the cat in the Grand Canyon. Ruby. Her name is Ruby.

It all makes sense to me. He's still in love with Ruby. That's why he's leaving Los Angeles. She broke his heart, and he can no longer handle living in the same city as her. Every restaurant, every street, every corner, reminds him of the time they shared together. He has never been enough for me because a piece of him is still with Ruby, will always be with Ruby.

Sean tells me that Ruby is cooking biscuits. I can see her pulling them out of the oven, red mitts, and blonde hair, out of a fairy tale.

I hear Jesse ask if he can come over. If she has extra. I am incensed.

"What are you doing?"

"It's fine," he tells me. "She lives close by."

I grab the phone from Jesse's hand. I tell Ruby she sounds lovely, but I'm very upset that Jesse read my diary and then immediately called her. Ruby is understanding. She tells me — and her voice is pure honey, so I cannot really fault Jesse for loving her — that Jesse doesn't subscribe to social norms, and I should not read into this. I thank her and hang up the phone.

"Why am I not good enough for you?" I ask Jesse. "Can't I be enough?"

"I'm hungry and need food."

I am hurt that he will take food from Ruby but not from me. I must feed him. "I will buy you whatever you want."

He says he has no cash, so I pull out a couple hundred dollars I keep hidden in a can on my dresser and throw it at him. I want him to have it all. I want him to pay off his credit card debt.

"What is this?" he asks. "Why do you have this much money?"

"It's my emergency cash."

"What's the emergency?"

It's cheesy, and I don't know if I mean it or not, but he wants me to say it, and it seems like the *Lady Bird* thing to do, so I tell him.

"The emergency is: I'm in love."

For a moment, I am. We are in high school, and we are coming of age, and he is my first, and I want him to deflower me. I am in the movies; my body is light. I straddle him on my bed.

He tells me that I'm his favorite person in the universe, and I don't believe him — because Ruby — but I don't care, and I'm crying again because I think that I'm no longer high and that I probably do love him, and I don't think it's fair that I'm not allowed to like someone and have it work out, but then I think maybe this is a first-world problem because look at me, I'm throwing cash at boys, and I'm white, and I'm privileged, and my family is not fleeing religious persecution or civil war. And it's MLK Day.

"Pizza," he interrupts.

The last time Jesse did shrooms, he ate pepperoni pizza. He tells me this as he goes to the bathroom. While he's gone, I want to surprise him, so I pick up my phone and call the vegan place near my house and order a vegan pepperoni pizza. When Jesse comes back, I ask if I should get two, and he nods.

While we wait for the pizza, Jesse dances a little more, this time with the cash I gave him. He asks me to take photos as if he has never held a hundred-dollar bill before.

He wants to give this money to the delivery man, to tip him a hundred dollars. The money was meant for Jesse — a token of my love — but because I'm so wise now, I understand that this money means different things to both of us, and if this is how Jesse wants to spend it, I can respect it. I also understand that a hundred dollars will probably bring the deliveryman more happiness now than it will bring me later during the apocalypse — cash will be valueless, anyway. So, I let him.

When the pizza comes, it's too much, and Jesse is confused as to why I bought two large disgusting vegan pizzas. He doesn't like the fake cheese.

"I'm just trying to make you happy without sacrificing my beliefs."

He puts down the pizza and picks up my laptop, "Can I read more of your diary?"

"You can't."

"Why not?"

"If you read the Sunday entry, I'll want to have a conversation," I say knowingly. "And I don't think I'll like what you have to say."

He shakes his head, "It's fine."

He opens my computer and reads. When he gets to the part about Spencer the lawyer, he doesn't seem as upset as I'd like him to be.

He puts the laptop down and turns to me, "I know you are dating other people."

"I only want to date you," I'm surprised by my honesty. "All of the other boys are just distractions. You don't have to move, I can provide for you, you can live on my bed forever and I will feed you and shelter you."

I'm rambling, but I continue, I like this fantasy. "And you can make music and date other people as long as you live on my bed. As long as you come back to me."

"I'm only dating you," is all he says, and then after a moment, "Can I make love to you?"

"Do you mean it?" The "love" part, I mean.

I can tell by his face that he doesn't, so I don't let him answer and pull him towards me instead.

I think that now that I'm so wise and know myself so well, I will be able to orgasm. But after a few minutes we both get too tired, and we just kind of lay there.

"I probably didn't mean all those things I said about loving you," I tell him, and then I ask him to lay on top of me.

It doesn't feel how I want it to feel, so we unwind, and after what feels like no time at all but is probably ten minutes, he tells me that he needs to go home and do his laundry. He doesn't want me to come with him. He needs to be alone. The fact that I need him with me does not seem to matter.

He gives me back the hundred dollars — the half he didn't tip — and I take it, because I don't want him to have it anymore.

He leaves, and I'm so sad now because even if he wasn't moving, he doesn't like to sit on the floor.

———

Tuesday, January 22, 2019

Dream Log: I skip work, and my boss assumes it was because I was interviewing for another job. Worried I'll leave, he promotes me on the spot! I'm a staff writer, making real money!

———

At work, I tell everyone I did shrooms, so now no one believes any of my three excuses. I hide in a conference room before I say something dumb about how I am forever changed

I am changed, though.

At lunch, I finally emerge and tell my coworkers the full story, Alexis tells me that she doesn't think that I love Jesse. She thinks that I was just on shrooms. I haven't known Jesse long enough to love him; I probably just like him a lot. Megan thinks that whether or not I really love him, I need to bring him to the end-of-season wrap party on Sunday.

I invite him, even though I don't think he'll be great in (any) social situation.

Per Alexis's request, I also ask Jesse when his birthday is. Alexis, who is very good at astrology, tells me that I'm not compatible with Jesse because he was born in the second half of November and not the first.

"You'll respect each other for your art," she tells me, one hand still on her phone, "but you will not work out long term."

I do not tell Jesse this.

When I leave work, my head is pounding. I'm worried that if I work out with this headache, I'll have an aneurysm, so I drive home and call Cheyenne. When I tell her that I tried to tell Jesse that I didn't really love him, she tells me that I can't take it back.

She also cannot get over all the shrooms I had: "An entire eighth? That's a lot."

———

Wednesday, January 23, 2019

I feel better today. When I drive to work, I put on NPR. I'm expecting to hear "Take Two" with Adolfo Martinez, but instead, it's "The Takeaway" with a new host. Today's episode is about the government shutdown leaving people homeless and how, because of climate change, a new animal is going extinct every month.

I turn it off. I miss Adolfo. He would have made some joke about it being "hump day."

———

Thursday, January 24, 2019

I forget to save the most recent version of my diary when I wipe my work computer, so a day of my diary is lost. I feel like I lost the day from my mind, too — my Word doc functioning as an external hippocampus.

I will try to remember.

Wednesday, I go to dinner with Jesse at a Southern Indian place in Hollywood. Afterward, we go back to his place so that I can look through some old shirts he no longer wants. Dev is at a meditation; Stella is maybe out of the picture.

Later, perched on a pile of old t-shirts, I ask Jesse to come over to my place and stay the night. I tell him that I like sleeping over more than sex, which shouldn't be a surprise.

I am first relieved and then enraged when he tells me he feels the same way, and that he only avoids staying over so that he won't get attached. I want to scream at him because it's not fair that he gets to protect himself when I'm already so exposed. He studied philosophy.

Doesn't he know this isn't right? But I don't scream at him, because I need so badly for him to stay with me.

I tell him, again, that I didn't mean it when I said I loved him.

He doesn't love me either. He's been in love before, that's how he knows. I don't ask if it's Ruby.

Hours later, when Jesse finally does come to my bed, he takes it over, spreading himself out diagonally, and reads from my laptop. He thinks he comes off poorly in my diary but does not expand on how. He is okay with it, he says. He corrects a few typos and tells me that there is really nothing going on with Ruby. He wanted Ruby and me to be friends because she edits books, but now that he thinks about it, he doesn't think we'd get along.

"You would like her, but she wouldn't like you," he tells me.

"Why?"

"She'd think you're the type of girl who works at Warner Brothers."

"I do work at Warner Brothers."

"Exactly."

I hate them both.

———

On Thursday I get to work late. I don't tell my coworkers why because there is no point in making excuses anymore.

———

Friday, January 25, 2019

It's my last day of work.

The day is sloppy, unhinged. I say goodbye to my boss three times — each time waiting in vain for him to confess how much my presence on the show meant to him. I steal three loaves of bread even though I'm not leaving yet, and gluten is bad for my thyroid.

I eat lunch two times and have the same conversation twice — about which Fyre Festival documentary is better — and come to different conclusions each time: Netflix, Hulu.

I think about stealing a computer mouse. I even go so far as to put it in my pocket and walk to my car, but I think about the karma so I run and put it back.

I delete everything off my work computer and return it. But I have work to do, so I work on Patrick's computer because he's already gone for the season. He never wiped it, so I text him.

Patrick: Go ahead. Wipe it all.

Once everyone else has left and I have filled my car with three bags of food that I don't want and a pair of scissors that were not mine to keep — yet somehow karmically less significant than the computer mouse — I finally find the energy to leave.

As I walk to my car I want to cry. This place has been my life for almost two years. If I don't cry, does that mean it has meant nothing to me? I look around the lot on my way to the parking garage, hoping to catch a glimpse of something that reminds me how much I've grown in the last two years, that makes this all mean something — a young girl on a golf cart perhaps, an empty bag of grapes flopping around in the wind. All I see is cement. One tree. I feel nothing.

The second I get in my car I forget about all of it. I think about the future. What am I doing tomorrow? What will I eat tonight?

Me: Will you come over?

Jesse: I am tired

Me: I just need a warm body in my bed

Jesse: I can do that

As I leave the gym, Patrick calls me to tell me that I have erased his entire Dropbox.

———

Saturday, January 26, 2019

I have a date with Spencer, the lawyer. I agreed to see him again because Jesse isn't enough for me.

I told him I'd take the subway to meet him — he's just read *The UN Climate Report*, so I thought it would comfort him — but I'm scared to take public transportation after dark, so I get an uber pool.

I probably should have taken the subway because I end up waiting, early and nauseous from the ride, in the lobby of Spencer's luxury apartment building. There is a Yale alumni magazine on the coffee table and a bored woman behind the front desk. She looks up at me.

"I'm waiting for someone," I explain.

After a few laps, Spencer pops out of an elevator. It takes me a second to get my bearing because he's shorter today and possibly more balding.

"You look nice," I tell him.

———

We end up at Baco Mercat, an upscale Spanish Mediterranean fusion restaurant with tiny twinkling lights strung along the trees lining the building. The last time I was here on a date the waiter told me I was going to die young and that I should drink tequila.

I drink tequila.

We order wrong but the food is still incredible. We don't get too much, so I don't overeat, and I don't bloat. The conversation is not memorable, save for the moment when capitalizing on my mistaken usage of the term "ghost-catching" instead of "gas-lighting," Spencer dives into a five-minute bit about the logistics of having a haunted house on the rental market.

It's not funny. So, for his benefit, I change the subject and start telling him about my recent shroom experience. He's never done shrooms — only weed, once.

I don't tell him about how I confessed my love to another man, though, because that does not seem like good date talk.

He pays for dinner, and we walk around downtown. I point out a few cool bars that are apparently too cool because the lines are impossible, and we end up walking all the way to Little Tokyo.

The walking sobers us up. I ask him what it's like to have such a generous disposable income. He's so immediate with his answer — "new" — that for a second, I remember that I'm talking to a real person. I feel bad that he is spending his hard-earned money on me. I do not deserve this. He is not really that rich. I'm not really that poor.

We finally make it into a bar, and despite not deserving it, I let him buy me another drink. The bar is loud, and in a back room there is large pit of men jumping up and down to Amerie covers. I want to jump with them, but I know that Spencer is not the right boy for that, so I settle for just nodding my head aggressively.

"I'm really tired," he tells me. "I think I'll have to call it after this drink."

Even though this is incredibly reasonable — it's almost midnight — I think that he must not like me anymore. I text Alexis while he closes out.

Me: He's a libra.

Alexis: You aren't compatible at all.

She sends a summary from a website explaining that I, the Capricorn, will not respect his emotions. I show Spencer the text and tell him that it's not going to work out. While he's looking at my phone, Jesse texts to check if I died on the subway.

We walk to Spencer's apartment, and he waits for me to call an Uber. This is the time to invite me in — to see his cats! — or at the very least try to kiss me, but my car arrives too soon, and he hugs me goodbye. There is candy in the Uber, so I pick out the red Starbursts, annoyed.

Jesse asks how my date was, and I invite him over because I don't know why he's asking these things, and my bed is cold again. When he comes over, I straddle him.

It turns out I'm very much addicted.

———

Sunday, January 27, 2019

The wrap party is tonight at seven. I have a lot of time to kill.

I walk three miles to Whole Foods 365 in Silver Lake so that I can buy beans in bulk. My mom bought me a crock pot for my birthday, and beans seem like the best way to eat real food without buying plastic. The beans are heavy in my bag. It was a bad idea to walk.

Spencer: Hey, what are you doing Friday? The cats want to meet you

———

I meet up with Sam and Alexis at Paloma, a club in Hollywood. Jesse is meeting me here.

The bar is already packed with our three-hundred-person crew and their plus ones. It doesn't make sense to be fashionably late when there's an open bar. I am in a grey knitted sweater dress – the same dress that I wear to every party – dressed down with orthopedic Clarks. I destroyed my ankle at last season's wrap party, I will not make that mistake again.

I'm overwhelmed, so I ask Sam to get me a drink while I collect myself in the bathroom. Now that I know I won't have to see him every day, I appreciate his unwavering cheerfulness.

I sit on the toilet and calm myself down. I'm worried about being sober around my coworkers, but also, I'm worried about being around them drunk. What if I blurt out something unappreciative about how our show is sexist, or mention that blowing up all those cars is bad for the environment?

I remind myself that the world is ending because that sometimes helps with my social anxiety. What I say at this party will not matter in ten years. My bridges are all going to burn down via wildfire, regardless. Or collapse due to our underinvestment in infrastructure.

I leave the stall. Now I am sad about climate change.

There is another anxious woman in the bathroom with me: Amber, a forty-something-tatted blonde in a white lace dress.

Amber cannot decide whether to keep her hair in a ponytail. Up? Down? What do I think?

I tell her to wear it down. I don't care, I just want her to stop fussing.

Amber tells me she loves me. She is very drunk.

I leave the bathroom. Sam hands me my drink. I don't like it — too smoky — so I down it while in line for another. The second one is better. It's tequila.

One of the upper-level writers is at the bar. He makes a joke about us having made out (the joke is that we clearly didn't), and I can't tell if it's made more or less appropriate by the fact that his beautiful (much younger) wife is within earshot.

"Joelle has a date coming," Sam mentions, as explanation for my nervously checking my phone.

The writer is confused: "Why have we been talking about sports at every lunch when we could have talked about who the assistants have been sleeping with?"

I panic. Maybe Jesse should not come. This is a lot of pressure for him: a room full of judgmental writers, light sexual harassment.

I'm about to text Jesse to tell him to wait until people are drunker, but just as I start to do so, he texts to tell me that his subway is stalled. Los Angeles public transportation is working out just perfectly for me. I relax and down my second drink. It's not a night to sip.

I'm mid-conversation with Megan and her boyfriend, working on my third or fourth drink, when Jesse texts to say he is here, outside. I rush out to get him.

I'm very excited and very buzzed. And when I see him, I relax, because even if I ruin things with my coworkers, now at least I have something else, someone else. I must make Jesse happy. I drag him into the bar. Before I let him meet anyone, I grab him a drink and load him with a series of appetizers that I could not eat — sliders, crab cakes, tuna.

Jesse talks to a couple of my coworkers, and other than one small mix-up where Alexis asks him if he's the Libra — "No, that's the other guy" — all goes well. Jesse says nothing about hating rich people, but even if he did, I would have been okay because the room was so loud, he would have had to use the mic for anyone to hear. Megan texts me to tell me that she loves Jesse, and I'm very happy, but also very sad. The night blurs. I'm as drunk as Amber.

When I realize that the DJ has stopped, I grab Jesse and drag him to a frozen yogurt place down the street. I add all the toppings that Jesse likes, so it's an inedible combination, but I eat it anyway. When we leave, I run to the subway, practically flying over the Hollywood Walk of Fame. My scuffed-up rose-colored Clarks kissing names that mean nothing to me, an entire world that means nothing to me.

I hold his hand.

When we get home, I have the spins, so I make out with him until I can see again. I don't really know how men's bodies work, but I think that if I have sex with him enough times, I will release some sort of chemical that will make him not want to move anymore.

———

Tuesday, January 29, 2019

I want food. I'm not used to cooking, and I have no groceries, so I scavenge my two shelves in the kitchen and make myself oatmeal.[10] I wonder how long I can go without salad.

---

10. Lunch at work was always provided for, and we had enough snacks in the office to tide me over for breakfast and dinner. Sam used to buy me four bags of grapes a week. In that sense, I was very lucky.

I work on that script Trey is paying me to help write, but after a couple of hours, I get bored. I need human contact. I try to call my brother, my cousin, and my mother, but my cousin is busy and no one else will pick up. I end up on the couch, and suddenly I'm watching some dumb show I don't care about, and Facebook is recommending a post about how Jesse is moving. Why does Facebook think that this is okay to show me?

I'm very, very sad. I cannot watch television. I cannot write. I can just lie on my couch and cry. I'm crying now.

It's 4 pm. On a Tuesday.

I look up therapists online, but none of them are in my area. I'm not so sad that I will drive an hour and a half to Santa Monica.

I look at my phone and see a missed call from my mom. I call her back.

"Sorry, I was gardening earlier when you called," she answers. "How are you?"

I tell her that I am crying on the couch in the middle of the afternoon.

"You always get like this when you don't have a job."

"It's hard when my job, my relationship, and the world are all ending at the same time. The thing I care about least is having a job."

"You liked your job."

I don't believe her. "Why do I have to keep prioritizing a career that doesn't matter?"

She thinks that TV is important. People need distractions, and the morals on my show are good.

"What morals?"

"There are strong family values."

I don't have the energy to correct her, so I ask her if she will at least agree that all the men in Los Angeles are horrible and shallow and that I will never find a guy I like again.

She will not.

"What about Gideon?"

"He has a girlfriend," I remind her. "You do not know what it's like here. I'm the one who has been dating in Los Angeles for three years."

"You can either see a therapist or come home, but I am not going to tell you that there are no good boys in Los Angeles. You are not a sad person," she continues, "you just get like this when you're bored."

Again, she is wrong.

———

I drive to my gym because I think that endorphins will help. The traffic is bad, so at the very least I will get to cry in my car. I put on a song I used to cry to when I was heartbroken in college — "Lose It" by Oh Wonder — and I smile because it's nice to have a constant in my life, even if that constant is sadness.

When I get to the gym, I don't feel good about running, so I just walk on the treadmill and text my roommate from college, Erin, whom I have not texted in a year. I tell her that she is making the right choice by getting an MFA in fiction. Television is stupid.

Erin: How is LA?

Me: All I do now is cry and write in my diary.

Erin: That's pretty much been my 2019.

———

Dad: u okay?

Me: Don't worry about me.

I think he should spend his time worrying about actual problems, death maybe? But I don't tell him this.

Me: I'm too sad to eat.

———

I go home and eat three slices of leftover vegan pizza, still mostly frozen, and then buy a flight home to see my parents. I guess this is not the type of depression where I get to lose weight.

———

As I eat the pizza, I call Cheyenne. She's upset about a boy, too. She's in D.C. for the winter, so she knows what sadness is. She tells me all the boys in DC are boring, and she can't date there anymore. I agree with her because that is what you're supposed to do when someone is sad.

———

Jesse: Excited to go to Little Tokyo tomorrow. ☺

I don't ask him if this will be the last time I see him, even though I'm thinking it. It's time for all my thoughts to be just mine again.

Me: ☺

———

Me: You up?

I have changed my mind.

———

<u>Wednesday, January 30, 2019</u>

Jesse: What's up?

Me: I wanted to ask you a question, but I am too busy now.

I'm mysterious and busy. This is ideal.

I have to drive to the Trader Joe's headquarters in Monrovia. Greenpeace is going there to drop off a stack of over 150,000 photos of people holding petitions asking the grocery store to go plastic-free. I don't know if my joining will justify the gas used to drive there, but I have the feeling that if I don't go to Monrovia, I will hate myself for it.

Also, I must stay too busy to text Jesse.

For a city I've never heard of, Monrovia is surprisingly close: just ten miles east of Pasadena. It reminds me a lot of Fairfield. The streets have potholes, and every store is a chain. I park in the lot of a 24-Hour Fitness and make my way to a group of people in the parking lot.

The Greenpeace employees remind me of camp counselors, maybe because they've all chosen to dress up like cheerleaders. One of the cheerleaders tells us all to stand in a circle and introduce ourselves: names, pronouns, organization. I'm hesitant to say I'm with Greenpeace because I clearly am not in with the "crew," so I mumble something about being new to everything.

"We're cheering on Trader Joe's, not protesting!" a cheerleader explains. "This action is nonviolent. If we're asked to leave, we have to."

Another cheerleader hands out slips of paper with useful tips about how to not get arrested: don't run, don't cover your face, don't wear sunglasses.

There is one kid present: Harper, who came with her dad. She looks about sixteen. She skipped school to be here. She knows that this – the environment – is more pressing than one day of her education.

I like Harper.

Meanwhile, a few Greenpeace members – wearing banana costumes – lead us to the other side of the parking lot, where we take pictures. I'm not sure what the goal of this outing is —other than the great pictures — so when I ask, one of the bananas tells me that they want to drop off the petitions and maybe get the contact number of the new Trader Joe's Head of Sustainability. Up until now, they've been in touch with someone named Mike, who oversees both sustainability and packaging — two very conflicting priorities.

With this in mind, we march down the street to the Trader Joe's corporate office, which is nondescript and surprisingly very small. The cheerleaders go in.

Thirty seconds later they are back outside. They didn't get anyone's number, and Mike was alarmed, so he kicked everyone out — but they did drop off the photo petitions!

We start walking back to the parking lot to debrief and maybe take more pictures when Harper runs back inside. She didn't skip school to leave empty-handed.

Most Greenpeace volunteers have left at this point, and I have nothing to do, so I stick around and wait for Harper. I talk to Donna, a member of the Sierra Club. She's friendly, probably in her late sixties, with short brown-grey hair.

I tell Donna that I was hoping to get arrested, and she tells me how she got arrested while protesting the Iraq War. She was put in a cell with a bunch of prostitutes in scrubs. She wondered, "Why are all these prostitutes doctors?" and then she realized that the police just made them change. I like Donna. A lot. I give her my number, and I tell her that I will join her club.

Twenty minutes later, Harper runs out with a Greenpeace leader and her dad. She's excited.

She tells us about her conversation with Mike, and how he justified all the plastic Trader Joe's uses. How this whole zero-plastic thing is just a fad. How they have to prepackage the produce, otherwise they'll have to install water sprayers, and those can carry diseases. Plus, they're expensive.

Harper tells us that she told Mike that using plastic is not an option: "Our planet is dying." I don't get to hear how Mike responded to that, because at this point the conversation shifts to whether Harper would like to be featured on the Greenpeace blog. (She would.)

I'm so proud of Harper that I don't think about how companies will never willingly phase out plastic.

I want to feel like I drove to Monrovia and had a win. And so, I let myself.

———

I'm supposed to meet Jesse at Starbucks, but when I shower and dress and walk out the door, I realize I lost my headphones. I go back inside and change because my clothing is too tight. I can't breathe. Nothing is right. I don't like what I'm wearing — it's stupid. Why do I even own a shirt with a dinosaur on it?

I try to tell Jesse I'm running late, but I forgot how to use my words. He calls me.

"I'm here but I can walk towards you."

I mumble, "okay," my legs will barely move. It is as if each blood cell in my body were replaced by a grain of sand.

———

After conveyor belt sushi and matcha ice cream, I'm normal again. Talking. Not exactly happy, but at least my legs work. I insist to Jesse that we walk to the Pershing Square Station instead of transferring downtown.

I wonder if I secretly want us to run into Spencer. Why else am I guiding Jesse near his apartment? Maybe there is a part of me that wants Jesse to see what he's up against, a part of me that wants this all to go up in flames instead of slowly dying out, one ember at a time.

"This walk is maybe dangerous," I tell Jesse, "But I feel safe with you."

He kisses me quick, on the lips.

"I was joking."

"I know."

He gets weird and starts to say things about how he thinks that I think that I like him more than he likes me — I do — and that he doesn't think it would work out long term, and that's why he feels a little better about leaving.

"That's such a mean thing to say!" I tell him, holding back tears.

"What? I thought it would make you feel better!"

I try to explain why it doesn't, but it seems so common sense that I have trouble coming up with a metaphor. I end up telling him that it's as if my arm is bleeding, and he tells me it's fine because we are never going to work out.

He is definitely on the spectrum.

He starts to cry a little, and it's nicer than anything he could ever say because his compliments always come out mean. He has hurt himself just as much as he has hurt me, or at least this is what he is saying.

"If I knew that someone liked me as much as I like you," he tells me, "I would feel really good about myself."

I try to take his hand and tell him that I like him that much, but it doesn't really land.

When we get to the subway, he hugs me all the way down the escalator. I don't fully enjoy it, because I have been ingrained with the importance of escalator safety, and I have to keep one hand on the banister in case we start to fall.

———

Back in my room, we both decide to be happy again. He wants a Tarot reading, so I pull out a card: The Queen of Cups.

"There is a smart, loving woman in your life," I tell him. "You have to treat her well."

He moves the cards aside and does just that. And, because I'm so loving and generous, I let him choose the music: the soundtrack to the Donkey Kong video game.

———

January 31, 2019

It's Jesse's last day of work so, he can't go in late like he normally does. He has to leave early. When I wake up, I'm shocked to discover that I'm alone.

It's pouring outside and there's thunder, so I stay inside and work even though I know I'm not supposed to write at home all day for mental health reasons.

At nine I see that Jesse has texted me, and I feel so good I do a little skip around my kitchen table. At ten he asks if he can come over, and even though I'm so tired, I say yes, of course, anytime.

———

Friday, February 1, 2019

I meet with Trey at Café 101, an iconic Hollywood diner that was, of course, also featured in *Swingers*.

Trey organizes his silverware. After eight cups of coffee and forty minutes of banter — my dating life, his frustrations trying to sell a show — he's finally ready to talk about *Drunk U.*

"So, do you really want to write this thing?" he asks me.

I think, perhaps for too long.

"I do."

I have gotten very good about lying in entertainment. I used to tell the truth a lot, and it turns out that is a very good way to not get jobs.

"I need a distraction from climate change," I tell him. "I will be sad if I don't have something to write."

He nods. "That's good enough for me."

———

By the time we leave the diner, I've had five cups of coffee, so I'm euphoric for the first time in a while. The air quality is pristine! I feel so alive! I text Jesse that I want to work with him at a library, but in the meantime, I need to run up the mountain near my house. As I run, I reach my hands out towards the sun, letting in the rays. I'm so happy. I think I'm probably bipolar, but if I get ups like this it's worth it.

As I skip down the mountain, I pass a man with a ponytail dancing. I smile. You and me, dude.

———

Jesse meets me at the library. I work on my feature, and he watches some videos for school. At one point he grazes my leg and it's distracting.

Around five, I ask Jesse what time he needs to leave. He panics and says, "right now." He is always like this, not realizing he has to go until I remind him. I think that maybe he would not have decided to move to Austin if I had not reminded him that he cannot afford to live in LA.

We leave and he drives me home, but before he does, he gives me a bathmat and a book titled *The Ethical Tragedy of Climate Change*. He cannot donate the book to the library because it's an advance copy. I do not want to read this.

———

<u>Saturday, February 2, 2019</u>

"What happened to the lawyer?" my mom asks when I call her on the way back from Lassen's, towing overpriced bulk chocolate (I am trying to make cookies).

"He just invited me out after the Super Bowl."

"That's nice."

"I said no, I'm too busy." Jesse is leaving in two days.

"Why don't you invite him to make cookies with you?" my mom suggests. "I don't want to bake cookies with him."

"It takes a while to start liking someone, you know, I didn't really like your father —"

"I know —"

"You should be nicer to men."

I suspect that she's just worried that I'm going to move to Austin for Jesse, so I tell her that I'm not going to move to Texas for a boy. Even for Jesse.

She drops it. She doesn't care who I date as long as I don't leave California.

———

Sunday, February 3, 2019

Jesse: Does nine work for dinner tonight?

I do not answer. Nine is too late. I'm insulted. There is no world in which I do not see him, he is leaving tomorrow, but I want to lie to myself for a while longer, pretend that I have the upper hand, that I could survive not saying goodbye.

I kill more time. My old roommate Nick is throwing a Super Bowl/Chinese New Year Party in West Hollywood ("Year of the Pig Skin").

I do not watch the game. Instead, I end up talking to another friend from college. I never thought we were particularly close, but suddenly we are talking about sustainability, his sick cousin, and how he is surprising his-long distance girlfriend in New York for Valentine's Day.

"I didn't initially want to do long distance," he tells me, grabbing one of my cookies, "She pushed. I'm happy now."

I look at him. He is happy.

Nick's girlfriend purchased dozens of paper lanterns for Chinese New Year. When the game ends, we all write our wishes on them and light them in the pool.

I write down health, happiness, less waste, more grapes. These are not really my wishes, though. I would like for Jesse not to leave me, and for climate change to be combated. Not in that order. Maybe in that order.

It's weird that I don't feel comfortable telling my friends just how scared I am of climate change. I am not sure they feel it the way I do. When I told Nick that I was sad that the world was broken, he said, "It's working for you, though, no?"

When we place the lanterns in the pool, the wind pushes them all to one corner. One catches on fire, and we watch the flames jump from one wish to the next. White paper burning in chlorine.

Eventually, Nick grabs a stick and moves the burning lanterns away from each other, but by then most of the lanterns have scorched.

———

When I get home, I cannot write. My fingers are heavy. My head is tired. My throat is sore. Even though I know Jesse will be here any minute, I decide to scrub my toilet with the bleach I purchased at a zero-waste refill stand.

Jesse calls while I'm mid-scrub. He is here. I tell him to go home. He turns around and walks down my stairs. He is good about playing along with my jokes. When I open the door, he walks back up my stairs carrying a bouquet of grocery store flowers.

"What are those for?"

"I just wanted to be nice."

I think because of rom-coms, and possibly also my childhood, I associate flowers with apologies, with grievances. Jesse has hurt me, either in the past or the future. The flowers are an omen.

"You can throw them away, they weren't expensive," he says, coming in.

"No. No. They are nice. Thank you. I don't have a vase, though."

I search around my kitchen and find a bright orange reusable water bottle. I shove the flowers into it. I'm being extra environmental, I think.

"Are we still going to dinner?"

Jesse nods. His car is packed. All his belongings Tetris-ed neatly in his back seat, the trunk. He pulls out a lampshade from the passenger seat.

"Can I store this in your apartment while we're out?"

I nod.

It wouldn't have been the most comfortable drive with him to Austin if he had let me go. If I still wanted to. Which I don't.

He runs the lampshade up and then gets back in his car. "Where are we going?"

I hate that I'm being made to choose. Like my deciding where to eat dinner will make up for the fact that I've had no say in his moving. I play it chill, though, because I still believe that I get my one ask — and I sense that I will have to use it soon.

I look at him and shrug. "This is your last night in Los Angeles."

He could go for a burger, so we drive to the Umami Burger down the road. It's closed. We go to the one in Hollywood. Other than logistics — where are we going, what is open — we have very little to talk about. Jesse is nervous. He's worried he's going to say something and hurt me.

"You will."

He gets more nervous.

We park. It's starting to rain. I have never seen Hollywood so empty. I like it better this way, abandoned.

"I think we should split two Impossible burgers," I tell him when we finally get inside, but he misunderstands. When the waitress comes, he asks for an Impossible burger and fries.

I don't correct him. I really don't care.

"I was so late to dinner because I had to say goodbye to so many people," he tells me. "I had to say goodbye to Jeff, Jeff's cat, Ruby. Jeff was sad that I'm spending my last night with you. It's a big deal, you know. That I chose to see you last. You should feel good about that."

He is being sincere. Trying to make me feel better.

"Mhm."

The only thing I feel good about is Ruby. Because even if he does love her, it's not enough to make him stay.

The food comes, and we split the burger. I ask Jesse about all his relationships, and he tells me about the girl he dated in college, a friend. He broke up with her, but they got back together when she insisted. And then she cheated on him.

"You're breaking up with me, too, you know," I tell him.

"I'm not breaking up with you."

"You are. This is a *de facto* breakup."

He does not agree.

The waitress drops the bill, and Jesse gives her his credit card. Even though I know he can't afford it, I let him pay. We are officially the last ones in the restaurant.

"We should write something nice on the bill," he suggests.

"We didn't even talk to the waitress; you can't write anything genuine on there that's not superficial." I refuse to let him rewrite himself as a good and earnest character in my life. He is just flexing for my diary.

"I guess that's true."

He writes "thank you" and we leave.

"If I were a waitress, I would want someone to write 'thank you, betch,'" I tell him. I feel better now that we're outside. I want to be fun again.

"Betch?"

"Yeah, but in the girlfriend kind of way."

"You're my girlfriend."

I'm flooded with panic. I ask him to repeat this.

"I guess, you're my girlfriend."

I'm thinking about my happy friend, the one doing long distance in New York. Am I going to be happy, too? I'm overwhelmed. My chest tightens. Do I even want this? Does he even mean this?

"What do you mean by girlfriend?" I ask, deliberately.

He shrugs. "I'm only dating you."

"Will I be your girlfriend in Austin?"

He pauses. Everything constricts. "No. Why are you bringing this up? Wasn't the plan just to date in Los Angeles?"

The tightness gripping my chest loosens, and I feel my heart falling, untethered, nothing to keep it in. I'm quiet. He is talking so fast I can barely keep up.

He's saying that long distance wasn't on the table. It never works. He tried it; it failed. We weren't going to do this. Is that what I want?

"Do you want this?"

We're in his car now. I'm nauseous. I feel congested in mind and body, weighed down by hundreds of simultaneous thoughts. I don't know which one is the right one. I do not know what I want. All I know is that I'm being dumped.

"You're not being dumped," he tells me.

But he's leaving, and he doesn't need me.

When he gets to my place, he tells me that he is going to find parking: "Is that okay?"

I passively let him. He's worried about someone stealing all of his stuff, so when he parks, I grin and tell him someone could definitely smash his windows in if he parks this close to the intersection.

He doesn't like this.

We sit in silence for a moment. It's still raining, lightly.

"Should I go home?" Jesse asks.

I don't like that this is even an option for him, so I do not answer for a moment and pretend to consider.

"I need to think," I tell him. "But you can come inside with me and sit on my bed while I think out loud."

He nods. He silently follows me in, slipping off his shoes. We sit on my bed, and I think.

I think about how his long-distance excuse is stupid. I tell him. Just because it didn't work for him once is no reason not to try.

He tries to interject, but I stop him. "This is my time. If you are going to dump me, I'm going to speak my mind."

He is quiet.

"I don't want to do long distance," I tell him. "But I don't want our relationship to end. I want to be able to call sometimes, and I want to be able to visit, and when I visit occasionally, I want it to be romantic. I do not want to visit you platonically. I do not want to be just friends."

"I want to be your friend regardless of the situation," he tells me. He likes me as a person. I hate that he is capable of moderation. That he can turn the passion off and still be able to think of me without mourning what was lost.

"I'm not done," I tell him. "I will not let you read my diary." He is quiet. I choose to believe that this silence is a sign that I have finally found leverage, so I tell him that he can either have all of me or none of me. "I've only been giving you some of me because you were leaving."

"What does that mean?"

"I don't know. But I think it sounds poetic."

I talk at him a little more — nothing of substance, nothing conclusive. But he agrees to my demands. We can stay in touch, and I can visit. And when I visit, it can be physical. Eventually, I get to a place where I'm still a little hurt but a lot more horny, so I sit on him until he asks to be inside of me. I tell him "No."

I cannot tell if I'm pretending or not. He has disappointed me so many times, and the only way I can possibly disappoint him is by withholding sex.

But also, I do not want to have sex thinking that this is our last time. I would get too anxious. If we don't have sex now, that means we've already had sex for the last time. This is all over with. I can move on.

"I'm going to be sad when I leave, too, you know," he tells me.

"Not for you, for me," he adds. He says this as if it is some global force separating us — famine, war — as if he has no agency.

I thought my career was stupid, but now I know boys are stupid, too.

And since nothing matters, I suggest we have sex standing up since I've never tried it before. He is too tall, so we do it the normal way.

Monday, February 4, 2019

I dream, many times, that Jesse has left, and that I've moved on with my life. He's still here, though, next to me, when I wake up. He asks me what I want from him before he leaves. I want him inside me, but we have no condoms.

I walk to 7-11 in the rain while Jesse sleeps a little more. I put a Starbucks cold brew and a pack of condoms on the counter.

When the cashier asks me if I need a bag, I shake my head and put both items in my raincoat pockets. I point to them: "Look, what a great jacket!" He laughs, and I'm glad he knows that I'm not ashamed of my sex life or my coffee addiction.

I wake up Jesse again, and because I want to set the mood, I offer to dance for him. He is impressed by my moves. The cold brew has made me very energetic, so I do a lot of jumping.

I get very tired, though, so I sit on the bed, sexy-like, and show him photos of every person named Ben that I've ever had a crush on. "Two of them have won Emmys." He thinks one looks like a douche, and I don't disagree.

I go to the bathroom, and when I get back Jesse is naked under my covers.

By noon, Jesse tells me he has to go if he's going to get ten hours of driving in. I walk him to his car, and he waves as I walk away. He calls my name, and I turn around. He is still there waving. I tell him to watch me, and I think he does because I hear my name again. I keep walking. I want to feel like I'm the one who is walking away from this.

I give a guy on Hinge my number and go back to scrubbing my toilet. There is a ring around the water, but when I'm done the porcelain will look good as new.

Why am I not more sad?

Part IV

<u>Monday, February 4, 2019</u>

The new boy from Hinge — Devin — invites me out for a drink. I know that it's very soon to go on another date, but the sooner I find love the sooner I won't have to think about Jesse. I also have been writing inside all day, fresh air will be good for me.

We meet late, at 9 pm. At a bar on Vermont, The Study. It's nondescript, dim lights, decent-priced drinks, and it's sandwiched between a large sports bar and an Indian restaurant. There used to be three bars in a row on this street — all connected to one bathroom in the back. It had been my dream to go on three dates at once, excusing myself at times from each to "use the bathroom."

For obvious reasons, this has never happened.

Tonight, the Study is almost empty. Devin is here, already nursing a beer. We hug, and he offers to buy me a drink. "Do you want something?"

"I'd take an orange juice."

"An orange juice?"

"Yes." I'm getting a cold. Possibly scurvy.

"I'm not going to order you an orange juice."

I don't need him to. I order myself one, and the bartender hands it to me for free. I know this bartender, but he is not creepy about it.

Devin tells me about his career, and I tell him about mine. He is doing well for himself punching up scripts and doing marketing consulting on the side but is not happy. I'm doing well for myself, assisting on a TV show and cat-sitting on the side, but I'm not happy, either. We will never be happy.

I tell him about *Drunk U*, and I complain about my inability to make it less sexist. He tells me that all comedies follow the same formula, and writers don't even make them funny anymore – they just add jokes later.

"Luckily my true passion is nonfiction."

"Is it really? That's very cool."

"No. I just say that to take the pressure off of entertainment."

"Oh."

He gets another beer. I launch into stories that I've told other guys before. The phrases roll off my tongue, memorized, and when he laughs, I cringe because he is laughing at the wrong things. These are not the punchlines. But I like that he is laughing.

———

"I need to finish the Ted Bundy documentary on Netflix," he says as he finishes his drink. It's been nearly three hours.

"Do you need to leave now?"

"No. Why? Do you need to go?"

"You just keep dropping hints about things you need to do."

"No. I'm just out of conversation. The Ted Bundy documentary was that last thing I could think to talk about."

I call it a night; run home in the rain.

———

Tuesday, February 5, 2019

"How's the drive?" I call Jesse on the way back from a meeting with Trey.

"What?!"

"How are you doing?"

"The connection is bad. I can't hear you."

"I know."

"What?"

"Where are you?"

"Huh?"

"Where are you?!"

"I'm in New Mexico."

"Cool."

"Yeah."

The call drops. I give up.

———

Jesse: I have made it to Austin

———

Wednesday, February 6, 2019

I have coffee plans with Donna from the Sierra Club. I feel awful. I am puffy and congested — hardly a state in which to talk about climate change — so I take two Sudafed and walk to an overpriced café on Vermont. The kind of place that sells CBD coffees for twelve dollars.

Donna is waiting in a loose-fitting button-down and holding a reusable mug.

"I would have brought mine, except I know this place has ceramic mugs," I tell her, nodding toward her mug. "I would never have suggested a place with only plastic."

She laughs at this, even though it is not particularly funny to me.

I am nervous — maybe it is all the Sudafed coursing through my body — but I want her to like me. She reminds me of the grandma I never had — brazen, bold, willing to risk arrest — but also of the grandma that I do have — warm, jubilant, layers of Coldwater Creek. I want her to take me into her warm bosom and tell me that it will all be okay.

She doesn't. She buys me a matcha lemonade and tells me about all the problems we are facing. She needs help fighting the largest urban oil field in the country, neighborhood drilling in low-income communities, and the tram Warner Brothers wants to build through Griffith Park.

"What are you interested in doing?" she asks, sipping from a hot chocolate.

I'm overwhelmed. Other than the tram, it all seems very dire, and to a certain degree fruitless, but that could be because my Sudafed is wearing off.

I pull out another pack and dry-swallow two more.

"Do you want one?" I offer. She shakes her head.

"I will do whatever you need me to do," I say, "but I probably cannot do anything for a couple of months because I am traveling all around the world."

She nods and tells me that an airplane uses forty gallons of gas per second. I do not fact-check this, but I make a mental note to stop flying after my next three trips.

———

By the time I get home, the Sudafed is at its peak, so I look at train tickets from New York to Austin. They're all miserably long and expensive. My friend Kamala did an Amtrak "Writers in Residence" program — where you get to ride the train for free and write — so I tweet at Amtrak that I'm writing a book about environmentalism and dating and I want them to help sponsor my lower-carbon journey to Austin so that I can maintain a long distance relationship without destroying the planet. It's a long shot. They don't respond.

———

Around six-thirty, I go to Hyperion Public to meet up with my old coworkers. I order juice again; this time it is not free. Megan is there. She seems surprised that I'm not sadder about Jesse, and I tell her that I am sad, debilitatingly so. "It's so much worse because everyone is constantly telling me how much they love him."

She clarifies that she liked him relative to the arm-diarist serial killer I described to her, whom she expected to meet.

"He's not that great," she says, pausing to look over the happy hour menu. "We should get sweet potato fries, right?"

I nod. I can find another Jesse, I think. I correct myself: I can't.

The rest of our coworkers trickle in, and we spend a good three and a half hours talking about what we've been doing since the season ended — making art, watching movies.

Apparently, I'm very behind. Patrick tells me I need to watch all of *Game of Thrones*, Megan tells me I need to watch *Green Book* (for the acting), and Trey tells me I need to watch *Futurama* and *The Sopranos* even though I make it very clear that I have already seen most of *Futurama*.

This is so much content. So much time. When the world ends, I don't think I'm going to regret not watching *Futurama* for the second time. I think I'm going to regret not telling more people that I love them.

As the night progresses, my coworkers get drunker, and I get soberer. My third round of Sudafed wears off, and I'm pushing the medically recommended daily dosage. I call it a night.

Devin: I'm sorry for giving you a hard time about the orange juice. My friend ordered it tonight. I guess it's a thing.

Thursday, February 7, 2019

Dream Log: A nightmare. I'm flying to Miami during a hurricane. It's okay because the eye of the storm is closer to Fort Lauderdale.

I'm going home today to Northern California. It's only a forty-five-minute flight to Sacramento, and there are no hurricanes, so I think I'll be okay. When I board, half of the seats are empty. I think about what Donna said. If I hadn't purchased this ticket, would Southwest have canceled the flight?

Probably not.

My mom meets me at baggage claim and gives me a weak hug. She's happy to see me. I'm glad to see her, too, even though there is a layer of shame to this trip. I am here because I am too sad. Because I am a loser.

She looks me over. "How was your flight?"

"Bad. It was almost empty."

"That's good, no?"

"Well, according to Donna from the Sierra Club, a plane uses forty gallons of fuel a second, so no, I think it's way worse than driving."

"That doesn't seem right."[1] She signals for a full thirty seconds before merging right. She is a very cautious driver.

———

My childhood desk is littered with awards: student council, tennis MVP, valedictorian. I stare at them blankly. I thrived in the high school structure. Back when I thought that hard work would be rewarded, a future guaranteed.

My parents thought coming home would be good for me, but I'm already bored and lonely. There are no distractions and even though the dog loves me, he is not the same as a real person who likes me for who I am.

Around nine, I'm thinking of Jesse and how I miss him when he texts me to tell me he's wearing a shirt I gave him.

I remind myself that it's weird that he took a shirt that says "Future Mrs. Bortles" that I made for a Jacksonville Jaguars game. I drew lots of hearts on it.

Me: How is Austin? Are you excited about the new job?

Jesse: It's fine.

He used to text me paragraphs with annoyingly deep questions — "What is my deepest fear?" "What do I really want to do with my life?" — which I would then ignore because I thought they were stupid.

This is stupid, too. I don't know what "fine" means, really, and I don't know if I'm allowed to ask.

I bug my mom for melatonin because I want the day to be over.

---

1. It's not. A quick Google tells me that a 747 uses about 750 gallons per hour – which breaks down to about 0.2 gallons per second. But even this math is misleading, because burning fuel that high in the atmosphere is exponentially worse than burning it on the ground.

———

<u>Friday, February 8, 2019 — Fairfield, California</u>

Dream Log: I'm sexually harassed by another volunteer at my after-school tutoring pro-gram. He's the cute volunteer, so I tell him that he can harass me sexually, just not in front of the children. "Can you wait until we are done at six?" I plead. He cannot.

———

I spend the morning fumbling around and spilling things. It's not my kitchen, though, so I don't feel too bad about it.

I'm working on a packet of sketches to apply for *Conan*. I don't particularly want to write for this show, but this is the first packet my agent has sent me in months, and I don't want him to think I'm lazy.[2]

My mom and I watch some episodes for research. I don't understand why the co-host is also old and white. It seems a little repetitive. When I complain to my mom, she tells me that change takes time. Things are already so much better than when she was younger. I don't agree. We don't have time for progress this slow.

———

2. This is the standard process for applying to late night shows. The show gives you a writing assignment -- in this case, write four to five sketch ideas that would be good for the show -- and then your agent sends it in. It's rare that anything comes of it. Devin told me that he was called in to interview for Conan twice after writing packets and never offered the job. Casey has spent two years in Los Angeles just submitting packets.

<u>Sunday, February 10, 2019</u>

I go for a run. Past vineyards and horses and trees and rolling hills — green now but brown in the summer. I'm very lucky to have grown up here, and I'm very scared that this will all burn down soon. I pass electric pole after electric pole and silently curse PG&E.

The first time we evacuated our house, in tenth grade, it was an adventure. My dad pulled our birth certificates from the safe, and my mom told me to grab my valuables. I grabbed my diary and the most expensive piece of technology I owned: my T-84 graphing calculator.

We stayed at the Residence Inn at the end of the road, and I still played a three-hour tennis match in Davis, even though the air was thick with smoke. (I won.[3])

The second time my parents evacuated, I was not home. I was living in Los Angeles, surrounded by a different fire. My mom flew to Los Angeles, and I let her stay in my bed because my roommate was out of town. My dad commuted to work from a Motel 6 in Dixon. They both talked every day.

"How is the air?" she asked him, on speaker.

"You are lucky to be with Joey, honey. The air is so bad here." His voice was excited like he was narrating a sports game.

The summer camp I went to as a child burned down.

———

Jesse texts me and admits that he misses me. I feel better about thinking about him.

———

---

3. What I lost due to smoke inhalation; I will never know.

Tuesday, February 12, 2019 – Los Angeles

I hike with Megan and Alexis up to the Hollywood Sign. Alexis tells us that there are five different love languages: receiving gifts, quality time, words of affirmation, acts of service, and physical touch.

Megan's love language is doing favors. Mine is physical touch.

———

Wednesday, February 13, 2019

I have another date tonight with Spencer. We're seeing *Free Solo*, a documentary about a mountain climber. When I tell Cheyenne, she's shocked. "You're still seeing the lawyer?"

I put her on speakerphone while I throw on some layers: a maroon sweater, a thin puffy jacket, and a rain jacket. It's very cold outside.

"He's nice and remembers what I say." I am probably forcing this, but everyone I know is Team Spencer, so I will give him the benefit of the doubt.

Besides, he will be able to provide for me long-term, when the climate gets bad and the mass migrations happen. He is a safe choice.

I pause as I head out the door. "Also, now that Jesse is gone, maybe I will love him."

———

Spencer smiles when I arrive at The Study. "It's nice to see you." He goes in for a kiss, but I'm trying to scope out who's at the bar, so he ends up kissing my ear.

"It's good," he says.

"Kissing my ear?"

"No. The bar. It's a good vibe," he explains. "Do you want a drink?"

"I'm two weeks sober," I tell him. I read an article a few weeks ago about how giving up liquor for just a month can rejuvenate your liver. I need that. I have been drinking regularly since the first week of freshman year.

"So, no to a drink?"

I don't really want to be sober.

"I'll get the grüner." I like grüner because out of all white wines it tastes the most like water

"How was your weekend?" he asks once we've settled in a booth. He's gotten some sort of mixed drink. His clothing is neat and crisp. He must own an iron.

"I went home," I say, gulping my wine.

"You went home? What for?"

I can't very well tell him that my parents wanted me to come home because I was sad about a boy, so I just tell him about their dog. Dogs are a safe subject. I don't ask him how his weekend was, but I'm sure he hiked or something.

"I'm going to Michigan this weekend," I say, to fill an awkward silence.

"Michigan?" He seems somewhat hurt that I have not clued him into any of my travels.

"To see my grandpa. Did I not mention it?"

"No."

"Then I'm going to Europe, D.C., and Austin." I sip from my glass, it's empty. I don't like him more now that Jesse is gone.

"That's a lot."

I nod. "I may never come back."

"Never?"

"Ideally, I'll find love," I say. He chuckles, awkwardly. I know I'm being mean, but I can't stop.

I try to sip from my empty glass again and suggest we go to the theater just in case there is a line. There won't be one, but I'm too bored at this bar, and I know that if we stay, I'll keep saying hurtful things.

Free Solo is about a climber, Alex Honnold, who scales Yosemite's El Capitan using just his bare hands. Spencer keeps saying there is something wrong with his brain to make him want to climb up 3,000 feet of cliff without rope. I don't disagree, but mostly because I don't like talking during movies.

Alex keeps telling his girlfriend that he'll never give up climbing up rocks like this even if they start a family, even though he'll probably die. He is unwilling to compromise his lifestyle for her.

Spencer thinks this is awful. He squeezes my thigh. I don't know how to respond, so I just sit there. Alex reminds me a lot of Jesse. I understand why his girlfriend puts up with these things. I would follow Jesse around in a van if he let me.

———

After the movie, Spencer says he wants to do something, but it's after ten on a weeknight, so unless we want more alcohol there isn't much to do.

"You can walk me home?" I suggest with a yawn. "I'm pretty tired."

He nods. This will work.

"Thank you for coming out here," I tell him, trying to be nice.

"You came to me last time," he smiles. "It was my time to come to you. Plus, it was nice to take the subway."

"You could ride it back." My fists are in tight balls in my pockets. I don't want Spencer to try to hold them.

When we get to my apartment, Spencer awkwardly loiters for a second. I invite him up, but with the caveat that I'm very tired and do not really want him there. He is tired, too, even though he was not tired five minutes ago.

He calls a Lyft. It's three minutes away. That seems close to me, but Spencer keeps complaining about how long 180 seconds is, about how cold he is, about how bundled up I am. He is trying to hint that I should warm him up with one of my three torso layers, but I don't like hints. I like people who are direct, preferably because they are on the spectrum.

"Your ride is here." I point at a white hybrid.

He kisses me briefly, but only catches my bottom lip. I am too shocked to properly react.

As I go up the stairs I vow audibly that I'm done trying with him, and then go to bed.

I want to text Jesse, but I know he's asleep. I want to tell him that I think he's one in a million — which is really not that rare, but it seems accurate — and that I will never find another person like him again. I should stop trying. I want to tell him that I would follow him around while he climbs mountains and let him say mean things to me, but I don't.

———

Thursday, February 14, 2019

It's raining — an understatement, it's essentially a monsoon — and I have a date with my dermatologist to freeze off a wart. I purposely made it on Valentine's Day because I thought it would be nice to lean into the loneliness of it all — just me and my wart and then, hopefully, just me.

The appointment is quick and painless. On the way home, I listen to a story about the Parkland shooting. It's been a year today. A young high schooler is writing stories about all the victims.

"The children are so alive in my stories," she tells the host. "Sometimes I have to remind myself that they are still dead."

The monsoon is getting worse, and as I turn on Hyperion, my tires splash up water from a massive puddle. According to NPR, there is a flood advisory for much of the Southland. I did not know LA was in the "Southland," but I like it. It makes the city sound like a part of a larger ecosystem. The reporter warns about possible mudslides.

People are wrong when they say that California does not have seasons: we have fire and we have flood.

———

When I get home, I make a lot of food, even though I vowed to wait until noon to eat. I slowly start writing my late-night packet. I won't actually get the job, so it's hard to put too much soul into it. I'm mid-sketch when I see that Spencer has texted me.

Spencer: Hey, it was good seeing you last night, I've had a blast with you, and I think you're really smart, funny, and compassionate. But at this point I don't feel romantic chemistry, so I don't think we're the right fit. Good luck to you, Joelle, and have a great vacation!

I start to tear up, not because I'm particularly broken up, but because he didn't bother to wait until after Valentine's Day, and that seems particularly cruel.

I'm also angry. I have so much writing to do, and I can't be distracted by sadness today. So, I put my emotions aside and finish writing.

I tell Spencer that I feel the same way and that I also wish him luck. Then I tell him he should stop selling out. If he really wants to be an environmental lawyer, he should take the pay cut and do it instead of working at a firm that represents Exxon. He does not respond to that.

Me: I got dumped on Valentine's Day.

Cheyenne: This is good material for your diary.

It stops raining. I leave my apartment so that I can stop eating and start being more productive. It works. I work at the library, and then at a café.

I look at my phone on the way home, and it dawns on me that I'm waiting for Jesse to text "Happy Valentine's Day." I know I'm not his valentine, but he could at least text me that so that I feel less alone in this world.

I go to the gym. There's a boxing class at six, and I need to punch something. I'm early, so I just walk on the treadmill. I'm wearing the wrong pair of shoes, so I can't run. Now I think all these frivolous writing assignments and workout classes are a waste of time, especially given the fact that the world is ending, democracy is collapsing, and we are separating families at the border. I'm a useless human being.

I feel the world closing in around me. Not just our world, all the worlds: universes folding into one another, trapping me here.

I really need to punch something.

Normally this boxing class is taught by a coked-out boxing instructor who always wears too-tight cutoff jean shorts. But today there is a new instructor who was in the army once. He is short and disciplined. He wants to teach us form.

He's saying words I don't understand. I'm not extending my arms correctly, and I'm supposed to pivot something, but I'm not sure what. The bags are heavy and filled with what feels like cement. I'm annoyed. I didn't want to learn, I just wanted to hit things wrong and feel strong and sexy.

"Can't I use the soft bags?" I whimper. I'm worried I'm going to break my fist.

He shakes his head. "You need to learn how to punch correctly."

I look around the room, a garage-like space with mirrors on two walls. There is only one other person in the class. There is nowhere for me to hide.

I suck it up and use my brain. It does feel good to punch, even if I'm pivoting the wrong sides of my body and I'm too square.

By the end of class, I'm exhausted. I've forgotten it's Valentine's Day. I can barely move my back. I feel sexy.

Jesse: your diary is inaccurate.

I cannot believe that Jesse is texting me on Valentine's Day to correct my diary — which, yes, I sent him so that he would fall in love with me and my writing.

Me: What?

Jesse: you said that the climate change book I gave you was too cerebral for the library. Really, they couldn't have it because it was an advanced copy and was unedited.

Me: You're supposed to wish me a happy Valentine's Day, even if you're not my Valentine.

Jesse sends me an OutKast video. "Happy Valentine's Day."

I smile. This is somehow perfect.

I want to ask him if he still wants me to visit. I even write out the text, but I get nervous and delete it all. I really have to stop sending him my diary now, because I'm being such a crazy person.

———

Friday, February 15, 2019

My flight to Michigan is delayed. I sit at the gate and wait.

There is something about the gravity of flying, the impossibility of thousands of pounds soaring through midair, that humbles me. Everything about my life seems so trivial. I am just one of many; I have no control.

I tell Jesse that I want to visit. Probably on the fourteenth of March.

Jesse: You can visit anytime.

Me: But when is good for you?

Jesse: Whenever.

This is not incredibly helpful, but it's as close as I'm going to get to the right answer with him, so I feel satisfied.

While I wait to board, I get a text from Devin, the writer from a few weeks ago. I thought he gave up on me, so I was aiming for that thing where we mutually ghost each other because I don't have the heart to get dumped by another guy I don't like.

Devin: it's very hard to take you on a date when we're never in the same city

Me: Hey, I was here four days last week!

Devin: I'm not blaming you, I'm also out of town.

I'm choosing to see the worst in his messages.

When we board, the airline makes me check my bag, and I get nervous because I'm meeting my brother, his fiancé, and my cousin at the airport, and I don't want them to have to wait longer for me.[4] When I get on the plane, I see that there are bins and bins of overhead space. Fool me once, Delta.

But also, I know that in the scheme of things this small inconvenience will seem very frivolous when the airplane unexpectedly goes down, so I don't let it get me too upset.

I'm sitting in between the members of a large Portuguese family. I consider giving up my aisle seat so that the daughter can sit closer to her father, but I paid an extra fifteen dollars to be able to pee on my own terms. Instead, I sit with clear annoyance as they continuously pass a Costco-sized bag of M&Ms back and forth between the two of them.

When the stewardess comes around with the drink cart, she asks me if I want a drink. I tell her no, and she seems concerned. It's a long flight.

"I'm trying to reduce plastic," I tell her. "I'd take a half-empty can if there are any extra."

She comes back later with half a can of ginger ale and orange juice. I want neither, but after making such a big deal about the plastic, I don't think I can ask for a seltzer, so I take the orange juice and drink it all in one gulp so that it doesn't spill on my laptop.

———

I land almost on time.

After a frenetic car ride in which everyone talks over one another and my cousin works very hard not to crash the car, we arrive at my aunt and uncle's house in West Bloomfield

---

4. My brother did agree to let me come visit our grandpa together after I told him I
   cried about it -- again, just reinforcing the idea that if I cry enough, I'll get my way.

where dinner is waiting. My Bubbie is there, wearing a charcoal facemask, and I'm so excited to see her that I take a picture with her and send it to my mother. I want to keep her in the loop.

"You look beautiful," my aunt says, patting my arm gently. She's sweet in a way that I could never replicate because we are not related through blood. Sadly, none of her genes are mine.

"I'm on beauty pills," I explain.

"Beauty pills?" She combs her short blonde hair behind an ear, confused.

"For my acne," I smile awkwardly. "Spironolactone. I take it twice a day. It makes my face glow but also sometimes acts as a diuretic."

She looks concerned. Why don't I love my body more? "You don't have any acne."

"I don't *now*." It dawns on me that it's been so long since I've seen my aunt — around four years. She missed the entire period of my life when I had terrible acne.[5]

Grandpa comes up to me and gives me a hug: "Joey!"

I was dreading seeing him — worried that I'd have to face his mortality, which I am by no means prepared for — but he looks incredible. Like a thinner, considerably less evil Charles Koch. He is probably on a different brand of beauty pills. He moves his hands wildly as he tells me about his near-death experience in January.

He says he had a bad reaction to his chemo. His heart rate went up to 140 and his temperature to 103 degrees.

"I could have won a dancing competition the way I was swaying!"

The doctor told him to take a Tylenol, but luckily my mom drove him to the hospital right away. He was so scared — they were all so scared. Searching for an IV, the doctors destroyed all his good veins.

---

5. 2015 - 2018. Which just so happens to coincide with my move to Los Angeles, the most polluted major city in America.

"Bubbie, what a trooper! She stayed in the hospital room with me the entire time."

I wonder how many times he has told this story because he is very good at it. I wonder if telling the story helps him feel better about his brush with death.

Around nine forty-five, I notice that I have two missed calls from my parents and at least a half-dozen texts.

Mom: This is not funny!

Dad: Delete the photo!

Mom: Why is my mother doing blackface?

I call my mom: "Mom, it was just a facemask."

"It's never just a facemask!"

"No, a charcoal mask –"

"I cannot believe you took this photo." My dad pipes in. I must be on speaker.

"Dad?"

"Don't let this end up on Facebook. Delete the photo. Delete every photo."

"It's not going to end up on Facebook."

"It's going to destroy your career!"

"What career?" I mumble, hanging up.

My extended family is watching. They laugh, amused. My brother Michael is jealous: "Why do you get all the attention from Mom and Dad? They don't worry about my career."

———

Before we get ready for bed, my grandpa shows me all the ginger cookies in his pantry, and then makes me touch his spleen.

It's four times the size of a normal one, jutting out of his upper left torso, like an extra set of abs in the wrong place.

He's been a doctor all his life, but this is the first spleen he's seen quite like this.

———

February 16, 2019 – Bloomfield Hills, Michigan

I go with my grandpa to CVS. I watch as he signs for nine different prescriptions that cost nearly $300. "This one will last me three years, so that's not so bad." I do not say anything when the pharmacist puts them in a plastic bag.

"This is the granddaughter I mentioned," he says before we leave. "The one that writes for television."

An attractive pharmacist lights up. "We've heard so much!"

"Grandpa, how often do you come here?"

Another pharmacist answers for him: "This is his *Cheers*. He lives here."

———

Sunday, February 17, 2019

After breakfast — oatmeal, peanut butter, hemp protein — Bubbie shows my brother all the dishes he'll get now that he's getting married. Fine china. Glass serving trays. Blue vases. When I ask about what I'll get, she opens a small cabinet in the living room, full of plates wrapped in plastic.

"You'll get this when you're married," she tells me.

"What if I never get married?" I realize I'm acting spoiled, but I'm annoyed that I have to find a partner to get free shit.

"I'll be here for a while," she smiles. "You have time."

———

My grandparents lie in bed for an afternoon nap, and I lie on the carpet next to them in the fetal position. I have awful cramps.

My grandpa is worried, "Did you eat something?"

"I'm a woman," I explain. And that is enough.

He opens his nightstand and pulls out some 10mg hard candy. "Do you want some of my weed candy to help with the pain?"

I know that 10 milligrams are a lot for me, but my grandpa says he barely feels them, and his friend eats them by the handful, so I take one anyway. I'm four days sober, so I need something to take the edge off life.

"Just don't tell anyone I gave you these," he tells me. "Your mom would be upset."

Three feet away, Bubbie snores.

We put on a movie — a comedy with Owen Wilson. I laugh a lot but feel bad about it because all the characters are men. When I tell everyone that the movie doesn't pass the Bechdel test, [6] my grandpa asks if it was an exam at Harvard.

———

We're in the car now, and my grandpa can't figure out how to turn on his windshield wipers. The snow is coming down quickly, and I cannot tell what is road and what is snowbank. It's very possible that this is how we all die.

---

6. In order to pass the Bechdel test, a movie must have two named female characters that have a conversation about something other than a man. Very few movies pass. In fact, the show I worked on purposely created a character named Judge Bechdel in the second season so that we would pass, but we had to cut her for time.

When we get to my aunt's house, I stand in the snow as it falls around me like I'm in some sort of snow globe or Christmas special. They live in a suburb, but all the other homes feel so far away — warm cottages lit up in the distance.

I need to text Jesse. I'm not sure why, but I think he will somehow save me. Shake the suburbs. Drain my world and pull me out with tweezers. But when I pull out my phone, I cannot type fast enough. My fingers are too slow.

10mg is a lot of weed.

———

My uncle made brisket for dinner, and my aunt bought me lentils because she is thoughtful and knows that I am vegan. I pile my plate with lentils and then pile my lentils with salt. It feels like Thanksgiving.

We all gather at the table: my brother, his fiancée, my grandparents, aunt, uncle, cousins I barely get to see. We have never been together before in this amalgamation. I chide myself: I am going to ruin this reunion because I am so stoned.

I sit down at the table and shovel food into my mouth. But the table is too small. My aunt is so close to me. She's talking about the Oscar-nominated short films we just saw the night before at the Detroit Institute of Art. They were all so sad – comically so. Every film was either about a child dying or a child murdering someone. That's how you win an Oscar, I stop myself from interjecting.

I can get through this, I remind myself, if I don't say anything. One bite, two bites. The pile is unending. These lentils are not absorbing my high like I thought they would. Like I always think food will.

Oh no. I'm talking now. What am I even saying? Jokes. Dead baby jokes?! I am rash and loud, but I am funny. A part of my consciousness shuts off and suddenly I have transformed into one of any number of obnoxious white *Lampoon* boys I hung out with in college — using humor as a weapon and a shield.

I double down. I will continue to talk, fool everyone with my eloquence. Could a high girl make all these jokes?

I roll into a two-minute improvised set about how my grandparents called me fat.[7] My cousins laugh. I am being funny. I have fooled everyone.

"She's just being sensitive," my grandpa says, "because she's high on my weed candy."

"Grandpa!" How could he? This was our secret.

Everyone turns to look at me. "She's high?" The room sways. I've destroyed twenty-six years of mutual respect with one bad cramp and 10mg of THC.

My uterus feels wonderful, though.

As we clear the dinner table, I ask each of my cousins if my aunt hates me now. They all tell me the same story about how she got high once two years ago. I remind myself that I'm being paranoid, but that doesn't really help because when you don't trust your emotions you also don't trust the rational ones telling you to calm down. Dread grows.

I hide in the bathroom and take inventory of the beauty products on my cousin's sink: face soap, lotions, mascaras, toners, the infamous charcoal mask — plastic bottled consumption. I do not have the strength to reject a life like this, a life of denial, of privilege, of healthy skin. Not alone.

When I leave the bathroom, the incident has blown over. Everyone is staring, eyes glazed, at some sort of golf tournament on television. I sit down on the ground, next to my Bubbie. She looks down at me from her large armchair and starts telling me about the funeral she went to this morning. I stroke her hand as she tells me about pancreatic cancer and try not to look too high.

I want to be there for her, but I know I don't understand what it's like to lose all your friends. My mourning is existential. Hers is concrete. I could learn something from her, I think, about living with loss.

———

7. They did. My grandpa said that my brother was the "little sibling" not in age, but size, and Bubbie spat out her water when I told her that I weighed as much as Grandpa. (140 pounds.)

I try to sleep, but I'm too wired. I'm thinking cliché things about Jesse. I'm thinking about how I want to be a better person because of him, and I can't tell if I'm thinking this because I've heard it in a movie once, or if it's in the movies because it's a universal feeling used to describe love. But I'm thinking about it, and I feel dumb, and my heart pangs. I want to beat my chest.

———

Monday, February 18, 2019

My grandpa wants me to write a pilot about his life, so he tells me stories about Vietnam as I eat some oatmeal. He was stationed at the 126th field hospital in Korat, Thailand, as a medic. Because of visa issues, he got there late, and he missed the part where the officers had to clear out the jungle – full of mosquitos and disease. He missed the hard part. The malaria. The death. Well, most of it.

On his first day, he was sent to examine two bodies from an overturned Jeep. It was his job to decide whether they died in the line of duty. No one really died in the line of duty here, but it was easier to tell their families this canned message than the truth: that their loved one died being an idiot. Being a kid.

The pilot who flipped his plane trying to grab women's underwear off a clothing line? Line of duty.

Most of the men admitted to the hospital had venereal diseases. I laugh, and my grandpa's face hardens: "We also lost a lot of men to malaria."

He had a cast of friends. There was Dr. Credit, a physician who once made my grandpa do a skin graft alone while he was off with a prostitute, and then took credit for the entire operation. (Hence his nickname.) There was another medic, King, who fell in love with a sex worker and took her home to Rochester, even though he had a wife and children. She had a weird lump on her back that turned out to be leprosy.

He tells me about the commanding officer, Colonel Warren, but he does not say much about him other than that he was very sick with bladder cancer. The most exciting story, he tells me, was when Jessie Rankin, a female nurse, was showering, and someone peaked through the window to watch.

She was so angry that she made every man in the camp line up. "I can identify that Sonofabitch if I see him," she said. And she did. He was assigned to a base in Louisiana as punishment.

My grandpa slept in a bunk with twenty other soldiers, and the bathroom was a quarter mile away, through the forest and the snakes. If they did pull-ups in the bunk, they could see into the nurses' quarters, but no one did pull-ups because the nurses were not attractive. Except for Jessie Rankin. But she would catch you.

My grandpa was already married when he went abroad, and my grandma raised their two children in a motel in Arizona. All the men on the base hated Bubbie because she sent my grandpa dozens of Playboy magazines for him to pin up in the cabin, and as a joke she drew mustaches and arm hair on all the girls. When my grandpa came back home after a year abroad, she showed up at the airport with a blacked-out tooth and a pillow under her shirt.

My mom says that I am a lot like my Bubbie, and I think that sometimes she hates me for it.

———

I go with my grandparents to CVS to get more drugs. I think that I'm going to hear more stories, but instead, they just talk about the silver they need to get fixed. I have no idea what this means, but I assume they are cleaning it up for somebody's wedding.

When we get back, I'm on edge. My flight is tonight, and I feel like I'm just waiting to leave. I'm possibly PMS'ing from all the iron supplements I've been adding to my oatmeal.

I try to connect with my cousin that I haven't spoken to in years, but she gets mad at me when I tell her that she can't say that she is so poor that she has to use her dad's credit card to buy things.

"That's not what poverty is."

"You don't know me anymore. You can't judge." She glares at me from the kitchen table.

When she and my brother go to the other room, I don't follow. Instead, I sit with Bubbie as she shows me a card she got from a friend. It's a "season's greetings" card with two animated birds standing under some mistletoe. The colors are muted, and it strikes me as a very somber holiday greeting. Bubbie tells me that her friend is an artist, so when she received a store-bought card from her, she knew something was off. She shows me what her friend wrote inside — a final goodbye to my grandparents.

She died three days later.

I stop being so moody. I join my cousin and my brother, and we all lie down on my grandparents' queen bed. I apologize to my cousin. "I'm sorry for getting mad at you for saying you were poor," I say, sandwiched between her and my Bubbie's legs. "I was mostly projecting."

"That's okay," she tells me. She does not really think she's poor. She's going to start a consulting job in a month, anyway. "You should visit me in Chicago."

I have always wanted to go to Chicago.

Amtrak has not replied to my tweet, so I don't know how I'm going to follow through on my vow to never fly again.

————

Tuesday, February 19, 2019 – Los Angeles

I make cookies. They're mostly peanut butter and olive oil. I've given up on recipes. I'm off-book. While I wait for them to bake, I buy a flight from D.C. to Austin. I text my best friend from high school (Leela) who lives there, but I do not text Jesse.

When they come out of the oven, the cookies have melted into one giant rectangle. They are brownies now.

————

The flowers that Jesse gave me are missing from the kitchen. My roommate must have thrown them out. They must have been dead.

———

I take the train to Koreatown and walk across the street to a giant skyscraper that I think houses the Ecuadorian Consulate. The Sierra Club office is here, and I told Donna that I would come to a meeting.

The office is on the eleventh floor, a small grey conference room with a large table and a couple of filing cabinets. I open a drawer to find hundreds of tiny plastic shower timers.

"We can't hand them out because they are plastic," Donna explains.

The crowd — around ten people — is younger and more diverse than I had expected. There is only one old white man, Steve, and he is very nice and probably still in his fifties. Everyone else has a laptop, but no one has a Mac. I wonder if, ethically, I have invested in the wrong computer.

When we list our jobs and skills — everyone else is a lawyer or works at a nonprofit — I tell everyone I'm useless but that I could in theory type fast if I had my computer, which I don't. Donna tells me that I can be secretary since the position is open.

A few members speak about Los Angeles Unified School District endorsements — I already voted for the wrong candidate — and about oil drilling in Los Angeles. There are wells right next to schools, churches, and homes in predominately black and Latino neighborhoods. Some wells are disguised as buildings, and some are out in the open, painted green, in the middle of parks.

Kids are getting nosebleeds, asthma, leukemia. I feel oblivious and dumb. I remember once reading an article about how there are two Chicagos: the Chicago of the white and rich, and the Chicago of everyone else, marked by poverty and early mortality.

There are two Los Angeleses, too.

———

<u>Wednesday, February 20, 2019</u>

I'm too hyper from my oatmeal, so I go outside for a run. It's cold outside, and my ears are freezing. I think about turning back, but I don't. I jog slowly and listen to a podcast about Democrats running for president in 2020. I'm not sure how we are going to win this one. I'm not sure I really want to move forward in space or time.

I pass the library and look back at Jesse's apartment. I have a connection to that complex that no one else in this city does. No one else will run by Dev's door and think about a boy that broke their heart. I correct myself: possibly Stella will, but I get the sense that she is the one who left him.

When I get to the Shakespeare Bridge, I see that someone has drawn a large unicorn on a mattress and propped it up so that it looks like a giant canvas. I take a picture because Jesse likes unicorns. I do not send it.

I have a list of things I want to say to Jesse, but I don't send them because I don't want him to think that I'm thinking about him all the time. I still haven't told him that I have a plane ticket to see him. I haven't told him that I think he's one in a million, and I haven't told him that I don't want to date other people anymore.

I'm jogging up a sunny patch on Vermont when Jesse texts me. He's responding, days late, to my thanking him for a subway card.[8]

Jesse: np, bro

I'm not his bro. We have made love.

———

I get dinner with Devin the writer, but we end up meeting late, and I'm not drinking so I don't really allow myself to have fun. When he drops me off at home, we sit in his car for

---

8. When he left, he gave me his TAP card with a stored value of $100.

ten minutes and banter about nothing. I do not tell him that he is supposed to kiss me. I never see him again.[9]

———

Thursday, February 21, 2019

The boy in tech — Charlie Day — finally responds to my email asking him out:

Hi Joelle! Just wanted to take a casual 70 days to reply. Traveling a ton for work right now but would be great to hang sometime. If you're near the office, you should come by for coffee some Friday in March. Hope you're doing great.

Whatever.

———

Trey and I are supposed to meet in Echo Park, but I cannot find parking.

I circle the neighborhood three times and scream into the void. I'm low on gas. This is dumb. I take an unprotected left turn. If I get T-boned, I will not have to meet with Trey. It would be a nice excuse. Not death, but hospitalization.

I remind myself that I do not have to disfigure myself to get out of this. No one is really making me do this. Sometimes I must remind myself of these things.

I find a great parking spot.

Trey and I talk for a very long time — about my trip, about my career, and about his career. It is not until after we have ordered and eaten breakfast, some sort of egg dish, that he brings up the script he is in theory paying me to write. I tell him I'm traveling on Monday. I am going to Spain to visit my brother, and I'm stopping in London because somehow that's $400 cheaper.

---

9. I see him once more, in passing. He is with a girl and looks very happy.

"Then I'm going to D.C. for my other brother's wedding shower, and after that, I think I'm going to Austin."

He seems frustrated — he was expecting to keep meeting in person — but when I tell him I can change my trip he tells me to calm down.

It's bad for my entertainment career to leave Los Angeles. But also, time is short, I'm young, and the earth is warming. I should not care about my career. I should care about my family. I should see them now. Especially since my brother Robbie might move to Bali, and it's less carbon-intensive for me to visit him in Spain.

"Have you told Jesse that you're visiting?" Trey asks me, with a smile.

"Not really, no."

"You're going to move to Austin."

"I'm not going to move to Austin," I tell him. "There is a zero percent chance."

I correct myself: "Twenty."

———

Friday, February 22, 2019

My uncle calls me to say "hi" for the first time in years, and we get into a debate about how I'm a socialist. I get frustrated because if I knew I'd be teaching economics I would have prepared for this call.

I start talking about externalities, and how the free market doesn't account for climate change. He tells me that people are inherently good. I tell him that the system is broken. When I hang up, he messages me that I'm too young to be so cynical. I want to tell him that because of climate change I'm at least halfway done with my life, but I do not.

I'm frustrated and out of chocolate, so I decide to hike Griffith Park.

When I get up to the observatory, I look out at the view of Los Angeles and cry. The city is so beautiful. I can see hundreds of thousands of people from downtown to the Pacific, thousands of tiny cars, only tiny specks from here. But none of those people are for me. They don't love me, and they never will.

I think about the people I do care about, the ones that left, the ones that never moved here. I want to text them all, tell them all how much they mean to me. I think I should maybe stop hiking by myself in the middle of the day because I'm being crazy and dramatic and I'm crying so much in public.

———

I finally make it to the library to work. Just as I get settled, I see that I'm getting a call from an unknown string of numbers that I assume is my oldest brother, Robbie. He has not called in months — and I never actually figured out how to call him internationally[10] — so I pack my computer back up and take the call outside.

It's late there, and he's coming back from some sort of ultimate-frisbee party. He wants to let me know that his interview for the teaching job in Bali went well.

"They are going to make me an offer I can't refuse."

I can sense his smile. He used to live in Los Angeles. He went to UCLA and taught high school in Watts for five years. When I visited, he'd drive me to Manhattan Beach, and we'd park near Noah's Bagels and run along the water. It would be hard for me to keep up, but I'd try anyways. The sky was so blue, the sand so white. I thought how lucky he was to live here.

"You could refuse it, though, if you wanted?"

He corrects: "They are going to make me an offer that I won't refuse."

"Congratulations. Bali is really in right now."

"You can visit," he offers. His voice is uneven; he must be walking fast. He's possibly drunk. "Once I get settled, in a year or so."

---

10. When I asked for his international number, he told me it would be best if he just called me.

"I don't know. Flying that far is a lot of carbon." I keep my voice low. I don't want any strangers outside my library to think I'm one of those white girls who goes to Bali.

"You can stay for a while. Although," he starts to reconsider, "they burn garbage there. You won't want to see that."

"For energy?"

"No. There is nowhere left to put it. They burn it to make space. I'm almost zero plastic, though. You'll be proud of me. I think I produce about a bag of trash per month." I don't really know what this means.

"I am," I tell him. I look at the time. The library is closing in fifteen minutes. "I think I could come to Bali for a couple months. Maybe a year. I like LA, but all the people that I love have left. I don't know why I'm sticking around."

"Join the club."

"Huh?"

"Welcome to your mid-twenties."

———

After writing, I drive to the gym. At the stoplight, I give a homeless man all my cash — twenty dollars — and then burst into tears because who am I to feel good about myself when he still looks so sad.

———

Saturday, February 23, 2019

Me: My high school friend is in Austin and she wants me to visit the 14th. Does that work for you?

Jesse: Yeah.

Me: Okay, cool. I can stay with her too, if I'm too much.

Jesse: Whatever makes you happy.

Me: Maybe we can go visit the giant rock outside of town.

Jesse: Giant rock?

Me: I dunno. I've heard good things about it.

Me: It's really big.

Part V

<u>Tuesday, February 26, 2019 – London</u>

I arrive in London after a 10-hour flight feeling very happy to be alive.[1]

I'm staying with Kamala, my friend from undergrad. Kamala is confident and beautiful and has achieved most of my dreams already: Fulbright, book deal, Amtrak Fellowship. I'm not jealous of her, though, because her competency inspires me. We are in the jungle, and she is paving my way with her machete. I follow her moves carefully. One day I might do some of this, too.

I wait for Kamala at Gail's, a café near her townhouse. I order tea and a tahini bite and then pretend to work on my laptop. I'm too jetlagged to write. One table over, two friends talk about something mundane, their respective nights alone watching television. I eavesdrop, transfixed by their accents.

"Don't you love this café?" Kamala storms inside. She looks very cosmopolitan: tiny frame, green peacoat, wind-blown, long black hair. "It was perfected by two guys that work at McKinsey. Did you try the tahini bite? It's vegan."

Kamala's family is from India, but she was born and raised in New Jersey. She doesn't have a British accent yet, but if you told me that she lived here all her life I would believe you.

"I did. It was great. You're here early." I close my laptop and awkwardly try to extricate my suitcase out from under the table.

---

1. I spent most of the flight contemplating my death and whether I should give Jesse my Gmail password so that he can publish my book posthumously.

"My second professor didn't show, so I got to leave class early." She moves the suitcase aside for me, gracefully.

"What are you getting a Master's in again?"

She tells me and I immediately forget.

We leave Gail's. I look at her closer now. I have not seen Kamala in three years. Her gait is the same, but her face is thinner and her voice — aged. The veneer of youth gone.

"You came at a good time. I'm only here for a couple more months, and then I'm going to Kenya and then India. For reporting."

"My brother is moving to Indonesia." I try to sound worldly by association.

"Oh my god. I miss Indo. In Jakarta, there's an Obama-themed bar. They had a North Korea-themed bar, too, but they had to shut it down because it was used for espionage."

"Should I visit?"

"No. You wouldn't do well. The air is too gross, and you can't walk anywhere. Uber is a guy on a motorbike."

"Can I visit you in India?"

"I don't think you'd do well there, either."

———

We enter her townhouse. After I lug my bag up three flights of stairs, we lay on her bed and share a cookie. Her room is cozy, small. There's a desk in the corner, a tiny sink, a mostly bare wardrobe, and two giant suitcases.

"I have five outfits now," Kamala tells me. "When I left Jakarta, I had to pack my life into those two suitcases."

It's very possible that Kamala is a spy.

———

I shower, and then Kamala takes me to her favorite bookstore, Daunt Books. There is some sort of event going on inside — a book launch for a novel about pebbles — and wine is visible, so we walk in and pretend we belong.

Kamala grabs two glasses of wine. "Red or white?"

"I've been sober since Valentine's Day."

"You're in London on vacation. You can't be sober."

She hands me the white. I take it.

I turn towards the crowd of mostly old people. There is a lanky bald man talking into a mic. "Should we pretend to listen?"

Kamala shakes her head and leads me to the travel section and pulls out a book about Madrid. I should read it, she says, so that I know what to do when I visit my brother.

I shrug. "I'm not really going there to sightsee."

"What about Barcelona?"

"I think that if the world wasn't ending, I would write a travel book," I tell her. "But like, a fun one."

"Why don't you?"

She says this like it's easy, like I'm capable of anything. And maybe I am. Maybe it's just the wine and jetlag, but for the first time in four years, I don't feel like I have to stay in Los Angeles.

"Maybe I will."

———

I'm drunk, floating through London. Where are we? Marylebone? Yes. Marylebone. Kamala points to a row of Lebanese restaurants all owned by the same person and all named some variation of Marousha. "Which one should we go to?" I have no real preference, but I suggest we go to the second one because I want to seem like I have opinions.

We order a lot: hummus, labneh, salad, and a lentil-and-rice dish. It's a hefty spread, but we manage to finish most of it.

"We can do an intermittent fast tomorrow," Kamala says, finishing the labneh.

"I don't need to be skinny until Austin. We can eat well."

The jetlag has fully hit me, and I run out of things to say. Plates empty, we sit in silence. I'm worried that Kamala will regret inviting me here. Have I changed too much since college? Is it so obvious that I am no longer fun? But then she admits that she is sad about the man she was dating. They just broke up. She loved him, but she could not see him often enough to make it work.

"Can I see a picture?"

"I can show you one, but it's not important to me. I know it's cheesy, but when I love someone, I don't see them for what they look like."

I don't think it's cheesy.

———

Wednesday, February 27, 2019

Jesse: I got a cat. Her name is Wednesday.

I check the time difference. It is too early in Austin for me to respond, even though if I gave myself enough time, I could probably come up with a pretty good Abbot and Costello bit.

I feel less stressed about Jesse. If he does not want to text me, that's fine. I am busy. I am in London. I am too cosmopolitan to be desperate.

———

Kamala has class again, so I wander around. I'm wearing three layers — a shirt, a sweater, a jacket — but after ten minutes of walking, I'm too hot for any of them. It's close to sixty degrees. In February. I tie my layers around my waist and tell myself that this is normal.

When I get to Green Park, I see hundreds of people lounging around, enjoying the unusual warmth. I hear someone comment that it's the first day of spring. A gift. I want to scream at the couples picnicking, at the students reading in the sun, this is not normal! This is a warning!

But who would it help? Who am I to take this joy away from them? They probably know anyway.

———

When I meet back up with Kamala, she's also anxious. She tells me that she understands my climate anxiety. She wrote an article about going to Norway so that she could see the ice before it disappeared.

"I'll send it to you. You should read it."

———

<u>Thursday, February 28, 2019</u>

Dream Log: I'm on a plane flying through trash. It's very bumpy. Clouds of plastic in the sky.

———

It's dreary outside — proper London weather. I go with Kamala to her gym and we do a thirty-minute abs class with a trainer who once lived in Los Angeles. We stop by Tesco, after, to buy more nuts and coffee.

Grocery shopping in other countries used to be my favorite activity — I like looking at foreign sweets — but today I'm uneasy. I watch in horror as Kamala throws various items — apples wrapped in plastic, salad wrapped in plastic — into her cart.

"Can you buy anything with less plastic?"

"Not here." She throws some more plastic into her cart.

I excuse myself and go back to the gym.

————

Later, on the Underground, Kamala apologizes for commenting on my eating habits. She had told me that I wasn't eating much, and then I overate in front of her a few times to prove that wasn't the case.

Suddenly, I feel awful and huge. My mind is so impressive. One minute I'm stressed out about the fate of the entire human race, and the next, how many almonds I ate today (too many).

"I read an article about a woman who lost a ton of weight suddenly," Kamala tells me. "Men started hitting on her at parties and women hated her. No one believed her when she said she wasn't starving herself, but she was eating normally. She was just getting skinnier and skinnier. When she went to the doctors it turns out that she had a parasite."

"I don't like this story," I say, sandwiched between two men on the train. Their arms are stretched out wide. Regardless of how big I feel, I will never take up space like this — completely unaware.

"I think because we weren't gorgeous in high school," she tells me, "We were forced to develop great senses of humor."

"We?"

She raises an eyebrow as we get off the train.

"Okay, fine. All of my friends were considerably better-looking than me."

Kamala nods her head. I'm not sure she is right, but I'm also not sure that she is ever wrong.

———

We're in the makeup department at Harrods. Kamala is trying on some goopy eyeshadow.

I want to feel beautiful, so I ask a few saleswomen if they have anything to make my face look thinner. I'm fishing. I want them to tell me that I don't need to change. I don't need to starve myself or get a parasite. My face is perfect just the way it is. Beauty standards are white supremacist and toxic!

They don't. They tell me that there is no makeup to fix my face, but I can try this dark brown eyeshadow under my eyelashes. I do. Everyone agrees I look much better with it on.

———

For dinner (which I do not want to eat) we meet up with Kamala's friends at a Thai place in the financial district.

The woman works at a nonprofit — Save the Children — and the man does some sort of consulting to make sure that banks do not give out risky loans. They are both Australian. I do not catch anyone's name, and because their accents are so thick, it takes me a second to process what they're saying.

"How do you find Los Angeles?" the man asks.

I sip from my water, confused. "Umm... well it's a pretty large city. I think it's easy to find on a map."

He repeats himself slower, "No, I mean, how do you find it?"

It dawns on me that maybe he is asking me if I enjoy living there, but I'm still not sure, so my answer comes out like a question: "I like it?"

I slurp down some eggplant. I am an idiot.

"The anniversary of the tsunami in Indonesia is coming up," the woman saving the children says. "I'm worried about the press. We did a good job of collecting money, but the Indonesian government did a bad job of spending it."

"I donated to Yemen," I tell her, self-consciously.

"Save the Children does a good job there; your money was well spent."

I nod, relieved. I feel like I have passed some sort of test.

Her face is stern: "The situation is quite dire."

I do not have much to add, because I have not donated enough, but Kamala sells me well: "Joelle writes for television."

"Which show?"

I tell them. They have never heard of it.

"Season three opened in Aleppo, present day," I tell them. "Our main character ran around shooting men in turbans. When we asked one producer not to dress ISIS in turbans because it was inaccurate, he responded: 'but how will we know that they are bad?'"

They look mortified.

"I'm just an assistant. I have no power."

"I thought you wrote for television?" They are very confused now, so I explain that I do the work of a writer without the pay or credit, with the unspoken promise of being promoted one day. If the show does not get canceled. Which it probably will.

The man looks disgusted. "America has really mastered the art of unpaid labor."

"I mean, they do pay me." I don't like feeling like a victim.

"How much?"

"Sixteen an hour." I try to tell them that it's okay because I usually work sixty-hour weeks, so I get overtime. Sometimes even double overtime. But they still look upset.

———

Friday, March 1, 2019

At 5 am, my alarm goes off, and adrenaline gets me showered, down three flights of stairs, on the Gatwick Express, and to the airport two hours early. I get through security and stare at the breakfast menu at Nando's for fifteen minutes.

"Beans and toast?"

Jesse: Check out this picture of my cat.

His cat — who has been renamed Likho — is terrifying. She looks like the feline Miss Havisham. Maybe it's the quality of his camera, but her fur seems patchy as if she was left at the altar and has been rotting alone, ever since.

Jesse: Yes, she has a wonky eye but it's worse in person!

Jesse: Whoops, that last text was meant for someone else.

Ruby? I would be annoyed but I'm too worried about Jesse now. He must be so lonely. He's probably sent this picture of the cat to everyone as a way of reaching out for human connection. As much as I wanted him to hate Austin, I didn't want him to be unhappy.

Me: Are you doing okay?

He starts to text. Then stops. He is like his injured cat. Lonely. Unable to ask for help.

Jesse: My phone isn't working so well so it's hard to text.

Or maybe it's just all in my head.

———

It's sunny when I land in Barcelona, but it's allowed to be sunny, so I don't panic. It's the Mediterranean, baby!

I meet my parents at our hotel and instantly regress. I am spoiled, pampered, innocent. All the problems in this world are back on my parents to solve — what we are doing today, how we're paying for lunch, how I feel about my body, everything.

We wander around the Gothic Quarter, a maze of restaurants and tourist traps on narrow streets. There are some very old buildings. I don't know what I am looking at, and my dad is too nervous about my getting pickpocketed to let me look up what we're seeing. I feel useless; I'm walking around solely for the sake of killing time before the next meal.

Suddenly the narrow streets give way to a large square. Twenty-something young people are holding signs and chanting in Spanish. I join for a moment to see what's going on. It's a protest for the environment — these students want to save the planet. This should make me happy, but now I'm sad. I forgot for a moment that climate change was here, too. And this protest isn't nearly big enough. Don't more people care?

On the way back we get lost. I ask my parents if they want me to map the route to the hotel on my phone, and they tell me not to because we're wanderers now. We end up wandering a long way out of the way and then wandering a bit more on the way to dinner because we forgot where we made the dinner reservation.

We wander again, when my brother Robbie arrives, and eat dinner for a second time.

———

Saturday, March 2, 2019

I need coffee. I can't tell if the espresso machine in the room uses refillable k-cups or not, so I ask a hotel employee in the hallway outside my room:

"Excuse me, miss, are these k-cups reusable?"

"Qué?" She turns to me, patiently.

"Oh okay. Son los k-cup, reusable?"

"Quieres más café?"

"No. Plastica? Usar dos tiempos?"

She shakes her head.

"Um. Let me write in my Google Translate. Here. Does this make sense?" I show her my phone. I studied Spanish for eight years and lived in Argentina for two months. I feel so useless.

"Oh! No." She shakes her head.

"Gracias. Me gustan el mundo y los animales."

———

Dream Log: My parents tell me that they have a fourth kid, a baby named Owen. I don't care to meet him. I have two brothers who I like, and there is no space in my heart for a third. But Owen's not here. My parents left him at home with the TV on (Owen likes cartoons). Suddenly, I'm anxious. Is Owen safe? I want to meet him now. Will he be okay at home alone? Will we be okay? We are in an Uber racing home to check on him, and my seatbelt is covered in gum. Only it's not my seatbelt. It's the driver's seatbelt, and it's not gum. It's a human foot.

———

Sunday, March 3, 2019 - Madrid

The next three days in Madrid are what I expect them to be. Robbie goes back to work (he teaches at an international school with a gorgeous, modern campus), and we tour a series of museum exhibits that are also available in the States. We dine at a series of non-traditional Spanish restaurants because my brother has esophagitis, and Spanish food gives him reflux.

My dad has found some sort of Spanish guidebook at our hotel, so throughout the trip, he showers us with stories that are all slightly wrong because he does not have the best attention to detail.[2]

We're staying in Lavapies, near my brother's apartment and in what *Time Out* has declared the coolest neighborhood in the world. (The metrics by which they came to this conclusion are not clear.) It's close to the museums and filled with vegan restaurants and yoga studios. My brother tells me that it's gentrifying and admits that he is part of the problem. He is on an ultimate frisbee team.

Robbie is quiet, so to learn about his life we have to ask very direct questions. What do you normally eat? (A lot of beans.) How do you get to work? (The bus.) We learn the most about his life the night before we leave when we go out for Ethiopian food with his coworker, a tall confident woman who brings a bottle of Crown Royal to share and tells us all that she is essentially my brother's older sister.

She talks, which I appreciate, it keeps me from thinking about the last time I had Ethiopian food with Jesse. She tells us about teaching in Venezuela. About the corruption, the one safe hotel to stay at in Caracas. Whenever she flew home, police at the airport would look at the list of the people flying and call out the American-sounding names. Then they'd search through their luggage to see if there was anything worth taking. The smart girls would put tampons on the tops of their suitcases to scare off the guards.

———

"It's a very conservative country." She smiles.

"Was it easy to find tampons?"

"No."

I ask her if she'd ever come back to the United States to teach, and she shakes her head.

---

2. He points the street sign near our hotel -- Dr. Fourquet -- and tells me how, after his daughter died of Typhoid fever, the doctor drove around with his dead daughter's embalmed body and pretended that she was still alive. This is the story of a different doctor, and a different street. But close enough, perhaps.

"They don't pay enough," she says as she takes a swig of whiskey. "And I don't want to carry a gun."

———

<u>Saturday, March 9, 2019 – Washington, D.C.</u>

Two flights, one missed connection, and a train ride later, I arrive in D.C. Michael and my parents are engaged in wedding conversations, so I slip away to a sports bar in Dupont.

I'm meeting with a half-dozen white men from the *Lampoon* that I tried to impress in college. I am overwhelmed by their sameness. Most of them have read *Infinite Jest*.

They all think I'm doing well. I have found that when I'm skinny and my face is clear, people tell me that I'm doing well even if by all other counts, I am not.

I correct them. "My face just looks great because of my beauty pills. I am unhappy in Los Angeles. I'm going to move to the East Coast!"

"No, no no!" they all tell me. "Wait! We are unhappy here. We will come to you!"

I nod. Someone has set up a game of Jenga on the table, and we all go around pulling small wooden bricks out of the tower. It's anxiety-producing, a threat looming over the conversation.

One of the boys tells me that he is going to move to Los Angeles to work in television. He wants to hear my advice.

I try to answer honestly. "It's frustrating to work at a place where no one listens when women speak."

"Sorry, what was that?"

He was on his phone.

I repeat myself calmly: "It's difficult to work at a place where no one listens to the women when they speak."

"Oh yeah, I see that," he says, completely unaware. He thinks he is a good one because he tweeted all that shit about Trump.

"Pursue entertainment. You will do so well," I tell him.

"Isn't it hard for white men?" he says.

"Not once you get a job. Everyone will love you. You'll get promoted nonstop."

He nods.

It's very nice to see everyone, and I'm thankful that these people have made time for me. But I'm also hyperaware of how much testosterone and privilege is in this bar, how much testosterone and privilege I subjected myself to in college. I'm ashamed.

I tried so hard in college to make these people like me. I joined their club, listened to their jokes, modeled myself after them. I wanted them to respect me, laugh with me.

But now that I have worked with them — for them — I know I will never truly be one of them. I was wrong to care what they think.

When it's my turn again, I knock over the Jenga tower. The blocks scatter across the table loudly.

Sunday, March 10, 2019 – Washington, D.C.

I'm hungover and slow-moving, so I'm late for Micheal's wedding shower.

When I arrive, the trendy brunch spot is already packed – full of my brother's law school friends, his fiancé's family, my family.

I'm overwhelmed. It's rare for me to see so much family in one place. I station myself near the coffee cart and cycle through distant relative after distant relative. I feel like I'm speed-dating my own family, packing in as many updates and memorable moments as I can — forced, unnatural — before I get pulled away to someone new.

My future sister-in-law's family is calmer. She has two sisters and a brother, and they all live within driving distance of one another. This party does not have to be a big deal to them. I am jealous.

My brother has allowed me to invite Cheyenne to the shower on the condition that she buys him something from his wedding registry (She goes with a lemon zester, the cheapest item).

She arrives as the party is winding down and my four cups of coffee are wearing off. I have not seen Cheyenne since she visited LA in December, so I give her a big kiss on the cheek and make her promise that, when she gets married, she will not make me do anything fancy for her wedding.

"Oh, you'll be my bridesmaid," she says, walking towards the taco station, "and my bachelorette weekend will be us camping for two weeks."

"Okay, I guess that's fine."

As people file out, we sit at the bar on high stools and catch up about the new boy she is dating. She shows me his profile on her phone. I'm impressed. "He's cute, and he went to UC Davis. Smart."

"I know," says Cheyenne, "but look at these texts. He's trying to see me every night. He's *really* into me."

Hey, you around? You want me to make you dinner tonight?

Hey how's it going? I left my umbrella at yours, can I trade you a drink for it?

You having a good time with your friend? Need anything?

The messages are a bit clingy, but he seems cute, and over-texting is preferable to no texting.

I probe Cheyenne: "Do you think this is one of those situations where you don't want what you can have?"

She sips from her margarita. I can never tell if she is deep in thought or just drinks slowly. "Maybe. But that doesn't really change the fact that I don't want what I can have."

"Fair."

"What about your boy? What's going on with Jesse?"

"I don't love him anymore because he stopped texting me," I tell her without thinking. I have no idea if this is true or not.

"Let me see."

She scrolls through my phone, shocked. "You're barely texting!"

"I know."

"I mean, he's not even asking how you are." This is not helpful.

"I'm tired of trying to trick him into a long-distance relationship," I tell her. I do not want to trick anyone; I just want someone to want me for who I am.

"You should tell him you're upset."

I shake my head. "I have no right to be."

She disagrees. You always have a right to your feelings.

I'm sad when we leave the bar because I forgot that I'm alone. I was viewing Jesse in Austin as a sort of Schrodinger's cat — maybe he will love me, maybe he will not. But there is no box, and it's been clear to everyone for a long time. There's just a dead cat out in the open.

———

Monday, March 11, 2019

My parents leave for the airport, back to San Francisco. I don't have time to miss them because Erin (my college roommate getting the MFA) is coming over to my brother's one-bedroom (where I'm staying).

I was only expecting Erin, but Cheyenne shows up as well. "I thought you had work!"

"I'm working remotely," Cheyenne tells me with a childlike smirk. "Erin and I ended up staying up until three, so I slept through all my alarms." She makes herself comfortable on my brother's couch — my bed — and opens her laptop. "Should I send my first email of the day?"

It's 3 pm. Cheyenne hates her job.

My brother laughs. "I'm working remotely, too. It's a laptop party!"

I'm jealous of everyone's work-life balance. Everyone has a job; everyone has a life. Erin and Cheyenne got to bond without me, so they must not love me anymore.

I'm not good in groups of three. I remind myself that I have not seen Erin in over two years. She drove up here to see me and Cheyenne during her spring break, I should not waste our time together being petty.

I turn to her. She looks and acts almost the same as she did in college. Erin's always had a Rory Gilmore vibe to her, both in appearance and temperament: hyperliterate, proper, yet also very down to earth. She has short brown hair, a heart-shaped face, and a penchant for both literature and pop culture. She's from Dallas and went to an all-girls private school.

Erin is darker than Rory Gilmore though, because television is fake, and when you are as smart as Rory Gilmore, it's hard to be as happy. I wish that they would have warned us about that.

We were suitemates freshman year. After I told her that my brother had inflammation of his throat, we ran around campus screaming "espho-vagina." Senior year her sleep schedule got so messed up that she became nocturnal. I think she was maybe really sad.

"Erin, it's so nice to see you. How is Wilmington?"

I hover awkwardly over the couch. My brother's living room is not huge.

"It's good. You should visit," she tells me.

"Sure, is there a train from Los Angeles?"

"The only thing is that you'll have to bring your own water." "What?"

"We can't drink from our tap anymore because it's full of some chemical byproduct."

Erin pulls out her laptop and pulls out a news story from July 2016 that details how a subsidiary of DuPont has been dumping a chemical into the river upstream since the 80s. The chemical byproduct (Gen X) is linked to tumors and pediatric cancer. None of this is even illegal, because Gen X was not regulated by the government, because the government did not know Gen X existed. DuPont created it.

"That is so fucked. How do you brush your teeth?"

Erin shrugs. "Wilmington is bad for dating, too. All the boys on Tinder are in the army."

———

Cheyenne wants to show me her studio apartment. It's 6 pm, but because of Daylight Savings Time, the sun is still out. It's warm — sixty degrees. A beautiful day in a beautiful city. Erin and Cheyenne are beautiful, too. And now that I'm walking and moving, I tell them. I love them. I want them to know this now, while things are still okay.

My existential crisis is making me sentimental.

Cheyenne lives in an old rent-controlled building on the seventh floor. The elevator is tiny and slow. When we get to her door, Cheyenne pauses and tells me to keep my expectations low — it is a studio after all. But when she opens the door, they are more than exceeded. She has at least two feet of room between her bed and the couch. She has a bed frame.

And her bookshelf! She's got a very sexy bookshelf. It's full of books about feminism and climate change: Naomi Wolf, Naomi Klein, Bell Hooks. I pull off *Food Politics* by Robert Paarlberg. I forgot about Paarlberg — he was our favorite professor. He taught us all about coffee and cotton and food deserts and how he got fat in the Navy because they fed him so much. I remember that I wrote an essay about sugar subsidies destroying the Everglades, and then I was so angry at Big Sugar that I didn't shut up about it for over a year.

Cheyenne wants to take us to a brewery so we leave her apartment and stumble down to the sidewalk. For a moment, we all pretend that we are back in college, loud and silly. Cheyenne wants me to tell Erin about my shroom trip, so I tell her how I told Jesse that

I loved him, and then that I didn't really mean it, but then I sent him my diary anyways, so he probably knows.

"I stopped sending him my diary," I tell them, "Because he cannot find out that the lawyer that I was seeing to make him jealous dumped me on Valentine's Day."

Erin seems concerned so I try to explain that it was mutual: "I dumped him with my body; he dumped me with his words."

We get to the bar. The lighting is dark and it's not too crowded — but then again, it's a Monday. I order a sour.

I drink my beer while Erin shows us manta ray videos that this hot diver took in Australia. When she was living there, she met him at the dive shop, and they spent an entire day together before he left her at a bus stop and never saw her again. Erin does not have his number or his full name. All she knows about him is that he works on some island on the Great Barrier Reef and that he dreams about quitting his job and hiking in Nicaragua for ten weeks.

I tell her that she should go to Australia to find him, and if she can't find him there, she should go to Nicaragua and do a ten-week hike of her own. It will be a great book — *The Great Barrier Romance* — but instead of finding love, she can find herself.

"I already like myself," she tells me. "What I need is sex."

At this point, the woman next to us, a tall blonde with a tight ponytail sitting alone with a cheese plate, turns to us and admits that she's been listening to our entire conversation. She flew to Australia for a man once only to learn that he already had a girlfriend.

She smiles. "I like that your lives are also trainwrecks."

———

We end up at a ramen place. I am not hungry, but Cheyenne shares her ramen with me. "You need to eat."

We're quieter now, mostly slurping, and I'm sad.

Jesse is texting me. He wants to know what time I get in. If my friend Leela gets sick of me, he says I can stay with him.

My plan *was* to stay with him. I don't know what is going on. I don't remember who he is or why I'm visiting him. I don't know if he likes me, and I don't know if my liking him is contingent on him liking me, or if it's too late.

"What is your ideal outcome?" Cheyenne asks when I bring up the situation. I do not know.

I'm thinking about the opportunity cost of being in Austin. I like it so much here in D.C.

"You need to text him," Cheyenne tells me. She's right.

We finish dinner and call our Ubers. I think about what I want and about my stomach. I feel very bloated.

Me: What are your expectations? Do you still want me to come?

Jesse: I'm excited to see you. I like spending time with you. You are cool.

What the fuck?

———

Tuesday, March 12, 2019

Dream Log: I'm in Japan visiting Cheyenne. She makes me and Erin jump fences and commit crimes to fight some nebulous corrupt government. In the midst of a frantic getaway, I step in gum. Cheyenne doesn't think it's a big deal given that the police are on our tail, but Erin understands. I liked those shoes.

———

I look at my phone. I have a text from Jesse and an email from my grandpa explaining some joke that I don't understand. The joke concerns three women — a mistress, a newlywed, and an older woman who's been married for twenty years — who all vow to put on masks and long jackets with nothing underneath to surprise their significant others. It goes well for the mistress and the newlywed, but when the woman twenty years into marriage surprises her husband disguised and naked, he just asks her, "What's for dinner, Zorro?"

My grandpa says the joke has to be told from the point of view of a woman for it to make sense.

Jesse: What are your expectations?

Me: My expectations depend on your expectations, but I guess I will visit either way.

———

I meet my brother for lunch at his work, a nondescript government building with windows that don't open and stale dry air. His office looks like something on our television set. He has a large wooden desk and a closet where he keeps a suit, just in case.

A nervous-looking middle-aged man in a white button-up pokes his head in from the hallway.

"We're going to eat in the pod—" He recoils when he sees me.

"This is my sister. She's the writer, visiting from LA"

I try to shake his hand, but he's very jumpy.

"I'm taking her to the food court," my brother continues, "if you want to join."

He politely declines. He's going to eat in the pod.

I wonder if all this artificial light is healthy.

Michael explains that the pod is a conference room and takes me to the basement food court.

We walk by dozens of fast-food restaurants — including Starbucks, Subway, Qdoba, and Halal Guys — and end up at the salad bar at a small grocery store. I fill my carton with mostly lettuce because they charge by the ounce, and even though Michael is paying, I don't feel like I deserve the food.

Michael tells me that he was sad last night when our parents left, and I tell him that now that I have done shrooms I truly understand that it's okay to be sad.

"I saw the blood in my foot, Michael," I tell him. "My blood will always be with me."

He looks around nervously. He prefers that I wait until we are home to talk about illicit drugs.

———

When I leave, I get on the wrong subway and end up near the White House. As I approach, the wind whips my face, and my eyes tear up. I let the water stream down my face because I don't want people to think that I'm paying my respects to the current administration. I'm mourning the loss of democracy.

———

Wednesday, March 13, 2019

Dream Log: I fly to New York to visit Jesse, but he's busy so I'm stuck at his parents' house with his bedridden brother – who manifests as a cat. When Jesse finally shows up, he is not alone. He is with his fiancé! He's engaged! I am so angry. I try to hit him with my purse, but I keep missing.

Why didn't he tell me he was married?! I would not have come all this way to Brooklyn! I would not have watched his cat-brother! Why didn't he tell me?

He opens his mouth to defend himself, but I never hear what he has to say because I wake up.

———

I look in the mirror, disgusted by myself. My face is wide with stress and my stomach has expanded. My boobs are huge.

I leave the bathroom, resolved to never eat again.

"Do you want breakfast?" my brother asks. He pulls out a can of black beans. "I finished the beans, but I can make more."

"No thanks. I'm not eating today."

"But black beans are zero points?"

"I'm not doing Weight Watchers."

"Zero points," he repeats himself. How could I not eat something that's zero points?

"I'm good with coffee. Thanks."

"I'll just put them in the microwave, you can eat them whenever."

———

My brother has a dermatologist appointment a mile and a half away, so I walk with him. He's anxious about his wedding — not the marriage part, but the storage. He's been getting gift after gift from his registry, and it's adding up.

"Why did I ask for so much stuff?" he asks me, while we pause at a stoplight. He's walking quickly, it's hard to keep up.

"It is a lot of packaging," I agree.

"Why do I need to replace all of my perfectly good stuff with slightly newer stuff? My old blender is fine. I don't need a new one."

"I'll take your old blender."

"Well, no one has purchased the new one from our registry yet. I don't want to be without a blender."

"I don't think it will be very long."

"How about I buy you a new one? Here. I can get it on Amazon right now. A belated birthday gift." He pulls out his phone. "What's your address again?"

I am still boycotting Amazon, but who am I to stop him from buying me something?

———

After I leave my brother at the dermatologist, I run to the Washington Monument and then along the Mall. Outside the Supreme Court, I spot a bus full of high schoolers on a field trip. It must be so awful to learn about democracy at a time like this.

I take in the Supreme Court itself. The building is so beautiful. I feel like it should be crumbling.

I want to cry, but I can't. My music is too upbeat. And maybe it's for the best that I stop crying because the world did not react well to Tina Fey's *Saturday Night Live* sketch where she cries about Trump and shovels a cake into her face. Crying into a cake is a privilege. I remind myself that. I make a mental note to get involved with some sort of radical activist group when I get back to Los Angeles. I will pour fake blood on my body, if it helps, for the movement.

I decide to stop being sad. I make a list of the things I'm glad about. I'm glad that I never actually told Jesse that I think he is one in a million. I don't know if being one in a million even makes you a good person. The Magician was one in a million, and I regret dating him. [3]

———

I run around until my phone dies. When I get back to Michael's I finally eat the beans.

———

---

3. According to some random Internet forum, there are only 37,343 magicians in the world, and given a population of 7.53 billion the Magician is closer to one in 200,000.

"UC Davis boy wants to come over tomorrow morning to get his umbrella," Cheyenne says as she prepares a cheese plate for Erin and me back in her studio. "Maybe I will tell him that it's a bad time because my friend is in town."

"Isn't it supposed to storm this weekend?"

"Yeah. I don't want to see him, but it seems cruel to not let him get his umbrella."

"He can buy a new one, they're pretty cheap," Erin says. We all pass around a vape pen. I pour myself some wine.

Erin takes a chunk of brie and asks me what's the worst thing I've ever done. "Cheyenne and I already talked about this. It's a fun question."

I think for a moment. "It's hard."

I have so much guilt that I must have done something awful, but nothing jumps to mind. Haven't I witnessed a sexual assault? Stood back? Done nothing? I realize that I'm thinking of *The Kite Runner* and not about my own experience. But also, in a way, I have done all of this. I tell Erin that the worst thing I have ever done is the sum of all my privilege and inaction. "I should be saving the world. Look at me, I'm on vacation visiting friends and family, picking out all the fruit from this cheese plate."

"You did pick out all the apples," Cheyenne points out, slightly annoyed.

"Dairy gives me reflux."

Cheyenne tells me that my answer doesn't count. "I had a good one. I slept with a coworker and then lied to his wife about it."

Erin nods. "That is a good one."

I shake my head and eat the last slice of apple. "That's not what happened. You slept with your coworker when he was single, and then he started dating another girl, and if you overlapped you were not aware. Also, your coworker has never been married."

Cheyenne nods. "This is true." She works in solar, so she's already doing her part to save the world.

We finish the cheese plate and have nothing to do with our hands, so we all retreat to our phones for a while. Erin is on the apps again, or maybe Twitter. I do not know what Cheyenne is doing. I redownload Bumble out of boredom. (I deleted it about a month ago.)

Everything is still right there, just how I left it. All my information — my height, the picture of my legs — was still out there floating somewhere on the Interwebs. I look at my matches: Jesse is still there. Right at the top. His profile waiting for me.

I'm taken aback. He is so real to me now that I forgot we matched on Bumble. And maybe it's the weed, but something seems off. Different. It takes a moment for it to sink in. It's his profile. He has a new photo — a photo I took. Him sitting on a couch holding a cat. I work out the logic. He must have changed his profile since meeting me.

His answers are different, too. His profile is no longer a series of weird jokes about looking for a girl with good kidneys. Now it's a list of his favorite books — Borges, McCarthy, Jacobs — and a joke about how he quotes too much from the *2010 Honda Insight Owner's Manual*. Dumb but endearing. I can't even tell myself that his profile looks lame because his last photo is still him with an electric guitar on stage. He looks really cool in that photo.

I'm tumbling; my organs in free fall. The half glass of wine and the vape pen aren't helping as I fluctuate between self-hatred and despair. I'm a coin that someone has tossed into a well, constantly flipping. On one side: I'm angry that Jesse has moved on. On the other: I'm ashamed that I'm surprised, because of course he has! We're not together. And I think these two thoughts, one after another, over and over, in rapid succession — I am lonely, I am dumb — as I fall, deeper into the darkness.

I eat some of the graham crackers that Cheyenne bought at Trader Joe's, even though they are packaged in plastic and not gluten-free. I feel worse.

I can't tell Cheyenne or Erin about this. They will pity me. They can't pity me. I am thinking about the girl in the restaurant with the cheese who went to Australia for that guy. We are both trainwrecks, but I am the conductor, steering myself straight into this mess.

"Let's talk about this."

"What?" I look up at my friends, sitting on the floor around Cheyenne's coffee table.

"What are you going to say to Jesse?" Cheyenne says as if reading my mind, "Let's roleplay. I'll be Jesse; Erin will be his cat."

I try to change the subject to someone's career or something — didn't Cheyenne interview for a new job? — but they want to discuss how in two days I will be flying to Austin to see a guy who is already making me so upset.

"You shouldn't go," Erin tells me. "There are two options here, both bad. You will either get there and realize he's an idiot and hate yourself for ever liking him, or you'll love him, and it will be so much harder to move on when you leave."

"I know." I eat another graham cracker. "But I have to go for the story. For my diary."

What the fuck am I talking about?

Erin doesn't buy it. "What do you really want from him?"

I eat more graham crackers; a ball of dread grows in my stomach. I sigh.

"I bought the tickets when I needed to see him," I tell them. "I wanted more from him. But now it's obvious he's not capable of giving me what I need. But I don't know what I want, and I have the tickets now, and I already told my best friend from high school that I'm coming."

I double down. "I cannot blow Leela off. Female friendship is so important."

"You can go for Leela," Erin concedes. I know. I played that card.

I know that I'm being irrational. Leela will understand, and I have studied the "sunk cost theory." I do not need to get on the flight to Austin just because I paid $200 for a flight to Austin.

Am I going just for the ticket? Or am I going just because I told everyone in Los Angeles — Alexis, Trey, Casey — that I would?

"You can go for Jesse," Cheyenne tells me. "I support the trip. You can be friends with someone and still care for them romantically."

Erin is doubtful. "You can?"

"Yes. I'm doing that with AJ," Cheyenne offers.

"Yeah, but you live in the same city."

"And you're hooking up."

Cheyenne nods. "This is true."

I need Cheyenne to have all the information. Need her to tell me that I should go on this trip even though it's clear now that Jesse is a lost cause. So, I confess that Jesse updated his Bumble.

"He did?"

I nod. I show them.

"He should have unmatched you." Cheyenne is angry for me.

Erin is angry for all women, "Borges? really?"

"You should still go," Cheyenne tells me. "Nothing good will come. But you need the closure."

I nod. Nothing good will come.

Part VI

The Austin airport is bright and spacious. Everything feels crisp — vivid. I am happy.

I take a photo. I want to remember this airport, this feeling. I consider texting it to Erin and saying something about how this trip can't be that bad — because look, this airport! — but I don't, because the camera lens on my iPhone is too dirty and the short queue at Wok 'n' Roll doesn't really convey the euphoria I'm feeling.

At baggage claim, I see a couple embrace. I wonder how long they've been apart.

———

Leela picks me up at the airport in a Subaru hatchback. She's wearing burnt orange, and her hair is short and blonde. I tell her that she looks so Texas now, even though I'm not so sure what that entails.

She's getting a Master's in landscape architecture — again, very Texas — and it's more work than she expected, so she's probably going to have to stay in and study today.

"I also have a cold," she tells me. "We can do something fun tomorrow."

I nod. That's fine with me. I have plans with Jesse.

I look out the window while Leela gets on the freeway. It's very green. I'm always surprised by how green Texas is. "You came at the perfect time," she tells me. "The weather is finally nice again."

She swerves the car violently. "The drivers here are awful."

I want to repay her for picking me up from the airport (Jesse offered but had work), so we stop by a juice place, and I buy her juice and a reusable tumbler because it makes me feel better.

I tell her that I'm trying to do zero plastic, and she does not seem too surprised. She knew me in high school. She remembers all my boycotts. She did them with me.

———

I walk with Leela to her studio on campus, and she tells me about her project: a design for a water treatment plant. "There won't be a set route for people to walk on. People will just take whatever path down the hill offers the least resistance — like water. It will be ephemeral."

I chuckle at that last word: ephemeral.

"Did you just laugh at me?" She seems hurt.

"I'm sorry. I didn't mean to."

———

I have not seen Leela in a while. We were best friends in middle and high school. I always loved the story of how she ended up in Fairfield. Her mom was from Hawaii, her dad Wisconsin, and our shitty town was halfway between those two places. The plan was always to get out. This was unspoken in Fairfield – the plan for everyone was to get out.

Leela had a twin sister (fraternal) who didn't like me. "I hated everyone back then," she has since told me. "Do not take it personally."

I did.

All my memories of Leela are like water evaporating, on my mind for an instant, and then gone. Ephemeral. Us on a trampoline vowing to meet up as squirrels in the next life, us going skiing but then just eating bagels in the lodge, her laughing at me when I fell during a badminton match, lunch in the leadership room.

I visited her a few times at UC Berkeley, and she visited me at Harvard once, too. All my college friends called her Lovely Leela because she was (and is) gorgeous and nice.

I think we are both proud of each other. Like cousins, perhaps.

———

We walk to the turtle pond, and Leela points to the tower where Charles Whitman, a former marine, murdered sixteen people back in 1966. The first mass shooting on a college campus. I find it hard to believe that someone could shoot up a place with so many trees. Trees make you happy.

When I pictured the shooting, there was only cement.

———

I leave Leela with her work and go for a long walk to Whole Foods. When I return to her place — hot but content — I shower, shave, and wash my hair even though it looked perfect before. When I put on my eyeshadow, I can't help but notice that my eyes do look better, but my face is the same.

I don't know what to wear because I mostly packed for winter, and it's hot out. So, I chug some water and lay down on the couch so that I can cool off enough for jeans.

When Jesse calls, I miss it.

He's here, outside the door. Here. I should be more excited, but I'm too hot, too tired. It took so much time to physically prepare that I didn't have time to mentally steel myself. To panic.

I hold my breath as I open the door.

"Is Ben Shapiro Jewish?" he asks, immediately. He looks the same, except here he's lit up by the sun behind him, light bouncing off the green leaves of the trees. I am overwhelmed, not by his beauty, but by nature's. It is so strange seeing Jesse here.

"What?"

"I was listening to him in the car."

I shake my head, confused. I have no idea what he's talking about. I've never heard of Ben Shapiro, but I don't want him to know that. I want him to think I'm all-knowing. "He's probably Jewish."

He nods. "Is he the kind of nice Jewish boy your dad would want you to date?"

"Why are you asking me this?" I'm annoyed. This is not the reunion I was expecting.

He comes inside and gives me a hug, "Hi. It's nice to see you. Can I use the bathroom?"

I google Ben Shapiro while he pees, and now I'm upset I've heard of him. "He's married," I tell Jesse through the door. "My dad wouldn't want me to be a second wife."

When he comes out, I unpack my suitcase and toss him a series of gifts: Spanish chocolate, a mug my brother gave me, the scarf I got in London, and a bottle of wine that I bought at Whole Foods, just in case.

He puts his hands in his pockets and leans over me like a giant banana. "This is a lot. I'm sorry. I got you nothing."

"I didn't really buy this all for you. My suitcase isn't closing anymore so I can't take it home." This is a lie. I bought the chocolate and wine specifically with him in mind.

"Why does your friend have a painting of a can of Le Croix?"

"We're going." I drag Jesse out of Leela's room. He's being obnoxious. I did not think that I had expectations for our reunion, but it's becoming increasingly clear to me that I did, and that they were too high.

We walk to his car, and he tells me how he thought about saying something else to me as his first words — some sort of appropriation of the N-word. "What's up my –?" You get the gist.

I get mad at him, because he's white and from Arkansas, and he's not allowed to say these things, even as a joke. He tells me that his students use that word all the time.

"They say a lot of awful things. I have to choose my battles," he explains, pulling out his keys. This is unattractive. I look around, the street is empty. It's just us and the shade from the trees.

"You're supposed to be a role model," I tell him. "Did you have other possible first words?"

"No."

I don't think I had any first words in mind for him, but I would have been happy with him picking me up and spinning me around like the couple at the airport, or maybe just not mentioning my father.

His car is the same. The tank is still basically empty, and he's got the same generic Tums and hand sanitizer in his center console. His phone is new. His parents bought it for him it when his last one lost the ability to make calls.

"Maybe if you stop calling because data is too expensive, they'll pay for that, too," I tell him.

"That's an idea."

We sit for a moment in silence.

"Next week is my spring break," he tells me.

I swallow my annoyance. This would have been helpful to know before I booked tickets. "Are you leaving town?"

"Probably not. How long are you here for?

"I have a ticket for Wednesday." I'm irritated. Why is he just now asking? I try to sound nonchalant and busy. "I need to be back in Los Angeles so that I can cat-sit."

It is not lost on me that the only thing drawing me back to Los Angeles is someone else's cats.

"If you're around next week, we can go on a day trip," he says. This soothes me. I am less angry. "Maybe see that giant rock?"

"I would like that."

It's rush hour and traffic's bad, so Jesse suggests we stop by an anarchist books store on Leela's side of the river. "I've been trying to go for weeks, but every time I show up, they're closed."

"You think they're open now?"

"They should be," he pauses. "Also, don't tell anyone where I live. I have an image to maintain."

"I don't know where you live."

"South of the river. It's the nice part of town."

It dawns on me that I don't know his address or where he's taking me. My mom thinks I'm staying with Leela, so he could very well dispose of my body if he wanted to. "You've been playing the long con," I tell him. "Now is when you kill me."

He laughs. I feel a pang of nostalgia.

He parks the car in an empty lot, and we both get out. "It looks closed."

Jesse points to the hours posted on a window. "It should be open."

He tries the door. It's locked. All the lights are off.

I watch as he peers in, hands cupped around his eyes. "Does the anarchist bookstore always being closed when it should be open make you think twice about total anarchy?"

"It's only closed because the anarchists have to operate under the constraints of capitalism. If capitalism were abolished, the anarchist bookstore would thrive."

We get back in the car.

Waze estimates thirty minutes to Jesse's house. I start to ask a question, but Jesse doesn't want me talking over the GPS. I'm annoyed. Why does this artificial voice get precedence over me? But then Jesse makes a wrong turn, and then another, and our ETA doubles. Forty minutes to go two miles. I take his phone and read the directions to him. He's tapping his foot, and I can't tell if he is anxious about the traffic or about me.

I'm still holding his phone and directing him when a notification from Bumble pops up:

Jessica sent you a message.

A match.

I should be angry or hurt, but I'm not. I feel above it all. I have moved on. Dissociated completely from the situation. I have no emotional stake in this game anymore. I am a voyeur, watching Joelle squirm around in the passenger seat. She has to pee. I am fine. I have no physical needs.

So, when I bring up Bumble, it's not for me, it's for the girl in the seat, to give her something to talk about, to make the ride go faster, to take her mind off her bladder.

"You know what's funny…"

He doesn't take the bait, so I continue.

"I can still see your Bumble profile."

He looks at me, somewhat shocked, as I calmly tell him that he should have unmatched me. "It made me very sad [past tense, not present], to see you back on the apps, swiping and looking for love, especially since I have deleted all my apps."

He is confused. "How did you see my profile if you deleted all your apps?"

"I only got Bumble because I was high. I'm done dating other people. You're still my most recent match."

I see this land on him. His face morphs, frustrated. "Why didn't you delete your apps when I was in Los Angeles?"

As if my deleting Bumble sooner would have changed things.

"I was only dating to make you jealous. I told you that. You knew." Now I am frustrated again – both of me, the girl in the seat and the dissociated consciousness watching from above. Would that have changed things?

"I thought you were joking."

"I wasn't."

"I think you come off as joking a lot more than you think you do."

"I know." There's still a good twenty-seven minutes left in the car. I rack my brain for more transgressions that I can bring up to kill time.

We're on the outskirts of downtown, at an impossible light, trying to turn left to go over the river. The traffic here is always bad at rush hour, but the ongoing music and film festival (South by Southwest) isn't helping.

"I'm just on Bumble for the ego boost," he tells me, after a minute of silence. "Like I was in Los Angeles. It makes me feel less lonely. Most of the time I don't even go on a date."

He has told me this before, but I'm not listening. I'm looking at Jessica's profile. She's cute. Skinny. Blonde. She's messaging him about her favorite books (I hate her for reading!). And Jesse is asking her questions, he's engaging.

I'm jealous that she gets to talk to the version of Jesse who communicates. The Jesse who is trying.

"Your profile is pretentious and not funny. Borges, really?"

"You read it?"

"I don't think you understand women."

I start to look at his other matches. He gets uncomfortable and asks me to please stop.

"Why? Are you hiding something?" My words come out sharp, accusatory.

"No. You just seem mad at me."

I am.

We miss a turn. I forgot to read him the directions, so I cannot even blame him. This ride is unending. I am undissociated and can no longer pretend that I am separate from the part of me that pined for a complete idiot.

He starts to tell me about a short story he wrote a while back.[1] The story is about Elizabeth Cady Stanton and Susan B. Anthony traveling to the future with a time machine so that they can bring back a white man to explain that giving women the right to vote will not destroy the world. But when Stanton and Anthony drag the man through the time machine back to 1848, he somehow ends up naked. He's so hot and naked that they cannot resist having sex with him.

Jesse is objectively awful. I tell him this. "You are objectively awful."

"What?"

"Women do not just fuck everything that moves. Especially women on a mission to expand voting rights."

He laughs because I'm right. I think about Erin's prophecy. I'm disgusted by Jesse. What did I ever see in him?

Only watching him tap his foot in the driver's seat, waiting to make a left onto Lamar Road — I am struck by the urge to unclip my seatbelt and sit on top of him.

———

Jesse's apartment is normal. He has access to a swimming pool, a dishwasher, and a creek just behind a fence and over some railroad tracks. He has a parking space, and he does not have to move his car at 8 am because that space is not in a Bank of America parking lot.

His bathroom is clean, too. Unlike the one in Los Feliz, there are no stains, no yellow in the sink. The walls are white and immaculate, and there is a stack of *New Yorker* magazines on the toilet. I read one article by Jessie Eisenberg; it's not bad.

His roommate seems nice, too. She's a twenty-something Ethiopian girl who likes crystals, hangs tapestries, and owns a book entitled *14,000 Things to be Happy About*.[2]

---

1. Erotica, technically. He mentioned it on our first date, but I didn't include it in my diary because I was too embarrassed for him. Now I think he should be embarrassed.

2. The book is just a list of nouns. It tells me to be happy about eggbeaters, and I refuse.

If Jesse brought a girl from Bumble here, she would be comfortable. I remind Jesse that I liked him despite the impending murder, despite the fact that we had to walk by a sixty-year-old man doing yoga to get to his bedroom. Or maybe, that is why I liked Jesse.

"Are you happier now?" I ask him. He does not answer.

———

Likho, his cat, does not look like death in person. She is tiny, rat-sized, about three pounds — timid but playful. One of her eyes is clouded over, "wonky." That's why Jesse named her Likho. In Slavic mythology, Likho represents evil or misfortune and is represented as an old woman with one eye.

I hover my finger by her nose because Jesse tells me that this is how I will win her over. I must win her over. She is the key to his heart.

"Do you want to walk to the creek?"

I don't. I want to stay on his couch, and I want him to kiss me. I think about telling him, as I did on our first date, that it's time to kiss. But the stakes seem so much higher now. If he rejects me, I'll have to go home. And I can't do that because it will be expensive to change my flight.

We walk to the creek.

He asks about my writing. I tell him that the feature is coming along. I wrote act one on the plane.

"And your diary?" He hasn't seen it since early February.

"It's two-hundred pages now," I tell him. "It will have to end soon. Probably with this trip." I step over some rocks to cross the creek. "It's a lot of pressure, for something climactic to happen."

"You can make something up," he suggests.

"I could."

He thinks that the best ending will be for us both to lay on the train tracks together in some sort of weird suicide pact that has neither been set up narratively nor emotionally. As the train approaches, I will change my mind, choose life, and hop off the tracks, leaving Jesse alone to be crushed by speed and steel.

"I don't hate the idea of killing you off."

We are inside again, and Jesse is hungry. I suggest we have some wine (to relax), but Jesse wants real food. He hands me a stale baguette and tells me that there is some cheese and chicken in the fridge.

"It's hard to be a vegetarian in Austin," he explains. "I feel bad about eating animals. I know it's immoral."

I don't respond. Jesse starts to ask me a series of questions: How have I been while he was away? Have I been sad? Did he hurt me?

I shake my head, angry. He is not allowed to ask these questions without first telling me that he has been sad — no, barely functioning — without me.

"I'm *fine*," I tell him, appropriating his word. "I have been *fine*. I will be *fine*. I'm just thinking."

"What are you thinking?" He always wants to know what I'm thinking. Like he has a right to my thoughts.

"I'm thinking about the story you told. About the suffragists, and how even though I still think it's sexist and offensive, I was wrong to say that no woman is ever distracted by a male body in front of her."

Jesse shakes his head, confused. "I don't understand."

"It will make sense in prose."

"I'm going to set an alarm for a nap. If we go to sleep now, we can get in thirty minutes before the short you wanted to see." [3]

---

3. My friend from college has a short playing at the film festival across the street.

"I don't need to see it anymore."

"What? Why not? It's right there."

It has become increasingly evident that Jesse isn't getting the message, so I finally tell him what I'm thinking in a way that he will understand.

"I'm very horny," I say, "but also very worried that you don't want to have sex with me."

"You want to have sex?" he says, surprised. He's a complete idiot.

"Yes."

"In front of the cat? She's only three months old; she doesn't know what sex is."

I explain that I thought maybe we could ignore the cat, but if Jesse's using his cat's innocence to reject me, I would rather he just tell me. "I can go. I'll uber to Leela's."

I pull out my phone to prove I'm not bluffing, but before I can open the app, Jesse pulls me into his room and shuts his door, keeping Likho outside.

———

I hold his torso close. It feels so familiar. I have missed him.

I wonder if I look the same to him, so when I take off my shirt, I ask, "Do my boobs look bigger, I gained weight?"

"I don't know. Maybe you look the same? Do I look different?"

I don't remember. But he feels better than he did before. My body is tinged with longing, and his with having been longed for.

I realize that there are two Jesses: the physical one, here in Austin, who I do not really know and who I do not really like; and the imaginary one, who I have created, unknowingly, in my head and in the pages of my diary. But at this moment, they are one, intertwined together, reality and fiction, their touch incalculably better combined than apart. Jesse is both himself and who I have wanted him to be.

A warmth passes through my body quickly, and I feel my blood again, coursing with excitement. This is the perfect ending for my diary: the female orgasm. The sexually repressed anxious girl finally allowing herself to feel good. A sex-positive feminist finale to what I hope is not a reductive tale. But of course, now I'm thinking. I cannot stop thinking. I'm thinking that I'm being cruel to myself for adding all this pressure, and I'm thinking that I hate my brain, and I'm thinking and thinking, and before I can stop, it's too late. Jesse is done.

He apologizes, and I lay on top of him, still inside me. He is just one Jesse again.

———

Friday, March 15, 2019

It's early. I want Jesse to wake up so that I can tell him that I'm thinking of him. That I'm always thinking of him. Lusting for him and wanting him with every organ of my body — my brain, my heart, my ovaries.

I want to sing to him, songs by Brand New, specifically. I know this is dumb and childish, and I curse myself for having listened to pop-punk during my formative years because now the lyrics to "Moshi Moshi"[4] are running through my head even though the lead singer has been canceled.

But Jesse wants to sleep. He does not want to hear any of my secrets, even though they are all about him. It's unbearable. I get up and write on his couch.

After thirty minutes or so, he calls for me: "Why did you get up? Come back."

I do. I lay awake in patient thought as he snoozes his alarm. Once, twice. Three times he snoozes.

I want to extend my trip. Maybe if I stay until Sunday, I can convince Jesse to love me. I'm being crazy. He will never love me, and I'm not sure I need him to. The chemicals in

---

4. "Are you thinking of me, when you're putting on your make up, darling/ drying your hair like you do [...] You're wasting your time if you're trying to impress me, I waste all my time just thinking of you."

my body are tricking me. This is not how I feel. This is just the oxytocin fooling me. If I cuddled a rock enough times, I would have the urge to sing to it.

When Jesse is done snoozing, I finally tell him all my secrets. They don't come out as romantically as they did in my head, and I end up just complaining about having to walk by his old apartment by the Bank America parking lot on the way to the library. He tells me to take a different route and to get a cat.

I'm being too needy, he says, when I ask.

———

He goes to work, and I go back to sleep. When I wake up three hours later, I'm not horny or lonely or needy, or in love. I'm just hungry. I uber back to Leela's, and we get Mexican food. The menu has an entire section of vegetarian options.

———

Saturday, March 16, 2019

We're going to a free concert tonight, so Leela and I Lyft to her friend's apartment in the newly gentrified part of East Austin to pregame.

We have trouble finding the unit (they all look the same), but when we do, Leela's friend cracks the door open, holding back a dog. She's small and blonde.

"Sorry about the dog," she tells us. "He hasn't taken his anti-anxiety medication today." I wonder, but do not ask, what he's on.

Her apartment is spacious. A one-bedroom with a large living room and kitchen. I am jealous — of the space, of the anxious dog, of her ability to function in society – which I am completely projecting on her. "Can I ask what you pay for this place?"

She is excited to share her good deal, like her rent is a pair of jeans she found at a flea market: "1,100 a month."

"That's what I pay," I say. "I could move here."

"You should."

I consider. It's calmer here. I would be happy.

"Do you want wine? I have a lot of white and this bottle of Malbec that's been open for two weeks." She puts some bottles on the counter.

"Katie works in events, so she gets to take the leftovers," Leela explains. She is proud of Katie, too.

I take the old red wine.

More girls arrive. One girl brings chocolate, another more wine. Two show up drunk. They all have the same look — jean jacket, short blonde wavy hair — even the one from Wisconsin who works in cheese. They bounce around in a way that makes me think they have not read the UN's climate report.

One girl pulls out a Smirnoff Ice and downs it on one knee, laughing.

I cannot be fun with them. I know too much.

The girl who works in cheese starts talking about a party hosted by Rachel Ray. "Yeah, we waited in line for four hours, but it was worth it. Open bar. All this food."

"Your Insta looked incredible," someone remarks.

I do not want to be here. I want to be with Jesse, but he was not invited to the pregame. After I complained all morning about what a child he was, Leela thought it would be best if he just met us at the concert. I text him.

Me: We're going to head over to Lady Bird Lake around nine.

Jesse: Lady Bird Lake?

Me: The venue.

Jesse: It's a lake?

Me: I don't know. You live here.

I get more wine and wonder if not liking this group of girls makes me sexist.

But then someone asks me about my job, and I start telling them about entertainment. They are laughing at my stories. And they get it because they lived in LA before they moved to Austin. They lived this life, worked in entertainment — struggled to pay rent. It was hard for them, too.

They are happier now, in Texas.

I chide myself for feeling like I couldn't be sober around these girls, because now we're all laughing, and I'm eating the chocolate that they stole from the Rachel Ray party. It's good. They tell me that I am just like their friend Anna, who lives in Santa Cruz and has blonde hair.

Sometimes I forget that just because I'm so sad and existential it does not mean that I'm any better than anyone.

———

It's not a lake. Lady Bird Lake is a large field next to a river. It's gorgeous. The downtown skyline shimmers in the background. I count the skyscrapers in my head.

Maybe I'm capable of happiness here, too.

"I'm going to stay in town longer," I tell Leela. "I'm going to bail on cat-sitting."

She smiles and pulls me into the crowd, where all the girls are dancing in a circle. I'm not sure who's performing, but I don't mind bopping around in a circle. I check my phone.

Jesse: I'm heeeere

He spots me before I see him, swooping like a bird into my field of view. He's in his awful purple beanie and grey sweater. The colors are not flattering.

I introduce him to Leela and watch her face for any tells. Nothing. Leela is too nice. I am nervous. I want her to approve. I wonder if she thinks I'm too good for him. I told her this morning I was too good for him. I am.

"I'm going to go back and join the others," she says after a moment. It is awkward enough for me to be around Jesse, and I cannot imagine witnessing it as a third party.

We hang back. I'm tipsy, and he's hungry, so we walk around to all the food stalls: corn dogs, beer, shawarma, burritos. He opts for the shawarma and devours it. It's repulsive.

"Are you upset I'm eating a baby sheep?" he asks, yogurt sauce on his face.

I am, but I lie. I'm fun now. I don't complain about these kinds of things, "No, I'm not."

"I'm upset with myself," he tells me. "But it's very good."

He takes a bite and finishes it. "Can I tell you something weird about me?"

I stiffen. Didn't we already move past this? He continues, "I don't like concerts. They're loud and crowded."

I am unimpressed by this confession. "Concerts are stressful for a lot of people." I don't like them because they're soft targets.

"It's just weird because I'm a musician. I should like this, but I prefer house parties. They're more intimate."

I hand him my beer and try to change the subject to something more interesting. I am drunk and happy. "I may stay here forever."

"What about the cats?"

"I'll cancel on them."

"That would be nice. I'd like another friend."

I look at him, probably too intensely, and take my beer back. I didn't know that there was a wrong answer to what I said, but that was the wrong answer. He doubles down.

"If you're waiting for me to ask you to stay, I won't." He says this gently like I'm sort of caged animal, cornered and volatile.

"What. Why?"

"You're in a rare position in your career. You can't leave Los Angeles now. You have to see the TV thing through."

"It's weird that I have to live in Los Angeles to pursue a career that I don't want, just because I'm good at it."

"It's weird that anyone has to live anywhere."

I hate him.

———

We're walking now, back from some karaoke place. It's past midnight, and we've been walking for thirty minutes, trying to find some shortcut through the creek that should take us back to Jesse's.

"It must be somewhere over here," he says. We're behind an apartment building, checking the fence line for any signs of holes.

We're trespassing, but I'm too tired to protest.

"I'm sorry you're sad in Los Angeles," Jesse tells me. "You're my friend and I care about you. I don't want you to be sad."

It's unfair that when he's sad, it's attractive to me. But when I'm sad, he pities me. He shines his phone light pointlessly.

"Can we just look in the morning?" I ask.

We give up and take the long way home.

———

When we get back to his place, I pick around the chicken in his cold leftover Chinese food. In D.C., I told my brother that I could only ever date a vegetarian. I hate Jesse for making me a liar.

Jesse is too tired when I sit on him, so I get in his bed and ask him to play me the new songs he was working on about a rock and roll robot. I cannot handle how good it is — he is a *Flight of the Concords* character — so I put my earplugs in and go to sleep.

After the third song, he crawls into bed next to me and wraps his arms around me. Instead of being content, I think: "finally."

———

Sunday, March 17, 2019

Likho is biting me. Jesse is up, too, reading something and waiting for his allergy pills to kick in. (He's allergic to his cat.) I straddle him even though he's gross and congested. He wants to go back to sleep. He says he will give me one hundred dollars if I let him sleep. It's ten am.

I leave his room. I sit on his tan leather couch and work on my laptop.

Jesse's roommate comes out and introduces herself. Do I need coffee? I do. She has to go to work, but I can help myself to anything of hers in the fridge — two yogurts, some milk. (I am allowed to eat Jesse's food too, but I don't want any of it.) I feel a pang of guilt for laughing at her book. If there are 14,000 things in the world that make her happy, and if one of those things is an egg substitute, who am I to judge? All the things that make me happy — grapes, my parents' dog, coffee — also make me sad sometimes, because I know that they will not last forever. Especially if all the bees die.

———

Jesse wakes up at noon. "I want waffles."

"Okay. Where?"

He searches on his phone. "Waffle House."

"Waffle House?"

He sits up, excited. More excited about waffles than about the fact that I am in his bed, caffeinated and clearly suggesting we have sex. "You've never been? This will be an experience. It's a real cultural phenomenon!"

To pump me up, he plays me a country song about a man going to Waffle House with his gun after his wife cheats on him.[5]

Meet me at the Waffle House // It's goin' down // Just found out my ole lady's been messin' around.

Meet me at the Waffle House // And bring me my gun// Need someone to talk to before I hurt someone.

I try to match his excitement, but it comes out forced.

We drive for fifteen minutes and pull off the highway at what is best described as a truck stop. There is one hotel, one gas station and, next to it, one Waffle House. A beacon on a hill.

Jesse was right, Waffle House is a thing. The parking lot is completely full, and there is a forty-five-minute wait.

"The waffles are worth it," he assures me. There is no space inside, so we sit outside to wait. It's a beautiful day — blue sky, light cloud cover.

A waitress hands us a laminated menu and asks us to order before we are seated to speed up the process. The options are all permutations of three base foods — eggs, waffles, toast — in varying quantities. Nothing is vegan.

Jesse gets the chocolate chip pancakes. I order some eggs and Texas Toast and help myself to complimentary coffee. I'm starving at this point, so I add cream even though I know it gives me reflux.

Jesse doesn't have much to say this morning, so I get more coffee.

And then more coffee.

---

5. "Waffle House" by Colt Ford

The floors are sticky inside. "I'm being a good sport," I tell Jesse. I am giving so much of myself to him, sacrificing so many needs. At the very least I would like for him to acknowledge it.

He doesn't.

By the time we're finally seated at the counter, I've had seven cups of coffee and have completely lost my appetite.

The fact that we can see all the employees working does not help. There is hardly any space in the kitchen, and they all bump into each other as they fill plastic container after plastic container with ham and eggs "to go." One thirty-something employee has a strange rash on her forearm and a very sad green headband.

Oh yeah. It's Saint Patrick's Day. I forgot.

"Take a picture of me with my mug!" Jesse says, excited. This is an experience he wants to show off.

I take one, lazily without getting off my stool. The setting is gross, the subject juvenile.

"Do you want a picture?" he asks.

I shake my head. I would like to never remember this experience.

"I'm starving now," Jesse complains.

I have no sympathy for him. "You have brought this upon yourself."

He agrees but is still agitated. He swings his legs wildly on the stool, like a child.

When the food comes out an hour later, I eat it all even though I'm disgusted with my surroundings and myself. The toast is cold and soggy. I lather so much ketchup on the eggs that they are almost unidentifiable. I'm such a good sport that I want to puke.

———

We're back at Jesse's apartment. While he showers, I look into switching to an earlier flight home. There's nothing available. I consider sneaking on the top of an Amtrak car, but service from Austin to Los Angeles is unsurprisingly difficult.

I'm broken. And I suspect my sex drive is gone forever. I wonder if this was Jesse's plan all along.

———

Jesse is at a café, working on homework for his online librarian degree. I'm supposed to meet up with him, but even though I've gone for a run and eaten something that is not cream — an apple — I still feel gross. I'm overcome by a fleeting and irrational resentment for the public library system.

I shave my legs. I tell myself that I am doing this for myself. Not for Jesse. I put on a cute skirt and a green top. Again, not for Jesse, for me. I sense that I am the only person who will love me today.

The café is just across the street, but it takes me nearly ten minutes to walk there. I'm sluggish. My body knows what my mind will not accept. Happy-to-be-in-Austin-Joelle has reached a breaking point. The illusion can no longer sustain itself.

Nothing good will come.

After what feels like hours, I make it to the café and sit down across from Jesse at a table that is tight for both of us. The café is almost empty, so I suggest we move to a bigger space. But Jesse shows no signs of movement, so I pull out my laptop, and we work with our computers touching.

I have writing to do, and I'm trying to focus on it, but Jesse keeps interrupting me to tell me about things he's planning for us. We'll go to this museum and then that natural spring and then see this show. I wasn't expecting him to plan anything. I thought we'd just hang out, but he's got at least five activities planned for us per day. There's a museum he wants to go to, a cheap bar, and every night at dusk, bats fly out from beneath Congress Bridge.

"If you want to see the bats, we should probably leave now."

"I just got—"

I give up. "Yeah, sure. I can chug my six-dollar matcha." My gut fills with caffeine.

We're only ten steps out of the café when I ask him: "Did you plan so much so that we wouldn't have to have sex?"

He's surprised by this question. I'm surprised, too. I'm not usually so direct, but the passive girl in me died in Waffle House — drowned somewhere between coffees number five and six.

He slows down.

I watch his face for an answer, my brain still. I am present for perhaps the first time in my life. He turns his head down and mumbles, "I guess I did."

A dam is broken, the tension gone. There is nothing to stop the wave of anger from flowing through my body, drowning my thoughts.

My face goes hot. My jaw locks. My eyes well. I know that if I open my mouth for too long, a wail will come out, so I just ask him "Why?" and then quickly clamp my mouth shut so that the rage cannot escape.

"It wasn't easy to get over you. If we have sex again — get close again — it will make things harder."

He was getting over me? I feel set up. Tricked. It's not right that he gets to be over me when I did not even know that is what we were supposed to be doing. Getting over each other. I spent the last month holding on.

I cannot stop the rage from getting out now. Even with my mouth closed, it seeps out through my eyes, my ears, my jaw.

"I asked you how you were feeling. You didn't tell me this. You should not have let me come."

"I didn't think about it. I didn't know," a beat, "I probably should have thought about it."

"No shit." We're back in his apartment, now, and I'm crying on his couch.

I turn my anger inwards. I'm naïve. I should have known this would happen. I should have looked at what he said to me objectively, instead of selectively clinging to the minor things he did that gave me hope. My life is not fiction, and my trip around the world is not ending with love.

"I didn't say for sure that not having sex was the best option. I still have not thought about it." He's qualifying now because I'm that despondent, that pitiful. "Your question caught me off-guard."

And then I tell Jesse what I refused to admit to Erin, to Cheyenne, and what I refused to admit even to myself: that I came to Austin to show Jesse how great I am. So that Jesse would want me forever. I wanted to trick Jesse into loving me, into realizing that some of me is better than none of me. I wanted to do this in six days. At the very least I would get six days with Jesse. Because, for me, some of Jesse is better than none of Jesse.

If I had admitted to myself that this was my plan, I would have shot it down. I would have berated myself. I am a smart girl who protects herself. I am not a trainwreck.

"It's going to be hard for me," I tell him. "Whether or not we have sex."

He is confused. He just wants to do what is best. He's holding me now. He is looking at me. I'm looking at him.

We have missed the bats.

"Why do you even like me?" he asks, then immediately takes the question back. He knows that people often can't put into words why they like someone.

But I can explain. And then I do.

I finally tell him the list of things I never told him: I tell him how talented I think he is. That he is one in a million. That I will never meet someone so strange as him, so refreshing. I will never be moved to write pages and pages — an entire diary about someone — like I am with him. I always thought that love songs were just things people said, but now I feel them.

"I will never find anyone I like as much as you before the world ends."

"That's a good line. You should write that down."

"I'm not just saying it, I mean it. But now that I know we are hopeless, maybe I can finally move on."

"I don't like that word," he says. "Hopeless."

"It has to be hopeless. Hope makes me stupid. Hope got me to fly to Austin for a boy. If you told me that it was hopeless in February, I would not be here. I wish you had told me. I told you that when I came to visit, I wanted it to be romantic. You didn't question that. We broke up for good, and I did not know."

"I did not break up with you. It was circumstances. I moved. And what are the other options? Are you really going to stop dating guys in Los Angeles?"

I tell him that I already have. "I will pay for your flights, I will fly you to Los Angeles, and I will fly you back to Austin, and it will all be fine, and you would still be in my life. Are you really looking forward to dating strangers?" I ask. "You want to go back on these sad apps and swipe and swipe and swipe and disappear?"

He shakes his head. He is not on these apps looking for love. He is looking for a temporary respite from loneliness. Conversation. That was all he was looking for when he met me, but I just happened to be better.

"I do not need to find someone great again," he tells me. "Long distance won't work."

"Why won't you try?"

"I'm a nihilist. That means I don't believe in anything."

"I know what nihilism is."

"I know. I'm sorry."

If nothing truly matters to him, then he should let me have this.

"Do you love me?" he asks.

"I do."

I'm sitting on him now. I'm not sure how this happened. But I'm sitting on him and telling him how I do love him. Not shroom-love him. Real love. And I don't know how much of this I mean, or how much of it I just think sounds poetic. Good for the book. But I do not qualify it this time. I say it all anyway because I need to get it out.

I want him to know that all of me is his; all of my secrets are his. So that when he rejects me, it's final. There is no part of me that is still holding on.

I tell Jesse that I love him, and when I'm done confessing, he tells me that he is hungry. He would like to order a pizza.

———

I do not go with Jesse to pick up the pizza. When he leaves, I look on Hinge and respond to some musician that I do not care about and who, despite a week of vague conversation, I will never see in person.

When Jesse gets back, I'm disappointed to see him so soon. He brings me the pizza and a plate. I take a slice and eat the cheese first. Jesse thinks that this is odd, and I tell him that this is who I am, even though this is the first time I've eaten pizza like this.

I watch him chew, and it's disgusting. His mouth is full and entitled.

I look at Jesse and I shake my head. Then I nod my head. I realize I'm seeing the real Jesse, not the Jesse I love. I'm finally seeing his faults.

I do an inventory in my head: his front tooth with the cap that is slightly less white than the rest of his mouth. The weird haircut. The childishness, the meat. He is so proud to have worked in food service, but still gets impatient when he is hungry. He thinks he is so much better than people for being poor, but he is still so privileged. His parents still buy him a cell phone when his breaks. His needs will always come before mine: his sleepiness, his hunger. He is no better than any of them. He is still a white man living in America.

He is still just a boy.

"Am I going to come off as a villain in your book?" He asks.

"Probably."

As I pick off all the mushrooms from the pizza — even the slices I do not plan on eating — he tells me that I don't have to stay in Los Angeles. Moving to Austin just made him less stressed about money, not less sad. I'm not really listening though, because Los Angeles no longer seems so bad, even with the earthquakes.

———

Maybe Jesse was right that intimacy was a bad idea, because hours later when he changes his mind and is inside of me, it's not love. The electricity is gone. The music is jarring, my hips are throbbing. I'm exhausted. I'm not even anxious, just annoyed.

But when we are done, I like him again. When he talks about the movies he likes, he sounds smart, even after I remind myself that I hate when men talk about movies.

I wonder what the oxytocin has done to me because when I search his face, I cannot find his faults.

Eventually, I brush my teeth and floss and then get into bed next to him. He puts his arm around me, and I pull him closer.

———

Wednesday, March 20, 2019

The next few days are purgatory. One moment I'm in love. The next I'm angry. Trapped. He is a waste. I want him close to me. I want to change my flight and leave now. I want to never leave. I'm frustrated. Sexually tormented every morning while he sleeps, every night when what he can give me is not enough.

In the morning, I let him sleep in. I wake up. Write. Run. My knees throb in protest, and I look at the Austin skyline and reminisce about my college years in Boston. I was sad then, too. I tell Jesse this so that he does not feel so special. "I have always been sad, Jesse. This is who I am."

Despite his excessive sleep, Jesse is not a bad host. He takes me to Barton Springs and entertains me with fantasy stories and plays podcasts that I would not otherwise listen to. He shows me his favorite movies and his favorite short films, and our interests are complementary if not the same. He plays guitar — if not for me, at least in my vicinity — and we both sing to his cat, who seems to be in the middle of this fucked love triangle but clearly prefers my company to his. He drops me off during rush hour at a restaurant so that I can get dinner with a family friend — who, over a bottle of wine, tells me that I can be both sad and lucky at the same time.

We are intimate again, for the most part, but it is never like that first night. His potential is gone. Jesse admits that he has not dated anyone since me, but this no longer matters to me because he will date infinite girls after I leave. Every bar we pass is a new date spot. Every café some sort of meet-cute. I ask him if he will take dates there, or maybe there, and he shakes his head. There is a closer spot to his apartment. Within walking distance.

We finally see the bats at dusk, the night before I leave. I'm sad and quiet, and my blood sugar is low. We sit and wait with a crowd for an hour. As promised, when it gets dark, a few dozen tiny bats fly out from underneath the bridge. I'm not wearing glasses; they look like birds to me.

A young girl on the sidewalk near us turns to her mom. "We waited all that time for *that*?"

———

On the day that I'm supposed to return home, I sit on Jesse after a shower. He shakes his head, "no." He would just like to hold me close. Suck up my energy. He tells me how profound an impact I've had on him, even though it sounds condescending. He does not mean to condescend to me, he really does respect me — love me — even if it's not in the way that I would like him to.

I have forgotten that it's hopeless.

I give him a series of ultimatums. It's this or nothing. I won't be his friend. I can't be his friend. He nods, he understands.

I want him to get mad. I want him to emote. I threaten to leave for the airport now, an hour early. Steal his cat. Cut him out of my life entirely. Delete his number, his Instagram, his Bumble.

But he has already deleted me on Bumble ("That is what you wanted, right?"). I have nothing left to auction off. There is nothing I can do or say that will change his mind.

I got to the bathroom and blow dry my hair and eat a cookie, but I still feel sad. I'm filled with a sense of loss and hopelessness akin to how I feel about the planet. He was supposed to distract me from this, I think. He was supposed to make me feel less alone.

He is crying now. He tries to cover his eyes, but I see it. He blames it on the light from outside, but the blinds are closed. He says that he wishes he could be who I wish he would be, and I cry too now because I know that he can.

———

Before he takes me to the airport, we walk to the creek and finally find that shortcut he was looking for that night when we walked miles and miles. When we get to the other side, all the sushi from the night before suddenly hits him, and he's overcome by an overwhelming urge to shit.

He barely makes it to the public bathroom in time, but he does. While he's inside, I look out at the downtown skyline. I finally call the therapist back in Los Angeles that I'd been meaning to make an appointment with.

I take all the condoms when I leave.

Epilogue

<u>March 5, 2020 – Los Angeles</u>

When I get back to Los Angeles, there is no one waiting for me. Jesse does not change his mind. No close friend confesses their love — or if they do, I do not have the epiphany that they were right for me the whole time. The new boys I meet are mostly wrong, and if they're right, it's only for an instant. I do not trust them. I'm impatient. There is no time.

I think that I will never get over Jesse. Even though my friends tell me that I'm better than him and I agree. I forget his face, his body, his flaws, and I fall further and further in love with the memory of him. The creature I have created through my prose. I edit the pages of my diary, and my heart pangs a thousand times, a scab picked off so many times that I think it can't possibly ever heal.

Then it does.

———

Three weeks after I get back, I get an email about an orientation for a new environmental justice group. I almost miss it — a single line at the end of an email that I don't remember signing up for and normally wouldn't open: Sunrise Orientation Training this Saturday, sign up here.

I am not quite sure what an orientation training is, but the email says that they will give us the skills and tools to fight climate change. It will explain the Green New Deal and their plan to win. I sign up.

The night before, I come up with a list of reasons why it's okay to skip: It's all the way in Santa Monica. Eight hours on a Saturday. I have a date with an astronomer in the afternoon. I can't cancel that, he's cute. It's weird to leave early. It's not worth all the gas.

My excuses feel flimsy, paper fighter planes thrown at the ground. They pile up around me. I know that this is the right thing to do.

My job does not matter. Boys do not matter. I still have not found what is important in this world. Maybe I will at this training. Probably not, though.

I wake up early and take the bus.

———

The training is at a Universalist church off 18th street, in the suburbs. The sky is clear, and I can smell the ocean. It feels like another world. Beautiful. Calm. Baby blue.

"Sorry I'm late," I tell a blonde girl with round glasses and a "Green New Deal" t-shirt. I am out of breath; I just jogged the last three blocks.

"I took the bus and got off at the wrong stop," I explain while writing my pronouns on a nametag. I want her to know that I didn't drive.

She looks up at me but doesn't smile. Her hair is very short, her expression, owl-like – cool and intense. "You are right on time."

I go through the church and into the kitchen area, where breakfast is spread out on two foldable tables. Around two-dozen people ages seventeen to thirty-seven pick at peanut butter and grapes.

I stand next to the coffee and eavesdrop. Some of them are in college, some high school, but a lot of them are older, like me. One woman works at the Hallmark Channel, another in production. A girl with pink hair is graduating from UCLA in the spring.

A twenty-three-year-old in cutoffs and a crop top comes up to me and introduces herself: Lisa.

"Are you new to Sunrise?" she asks. She is loud and confident.

I nod and pick at a banana half. "I'm shocked that there is so much plastic." I gesture to all the containers, to the single-use silverware. "I've given it up."

I am so desperate to prove that I belong here.

"We are fighting the system," she tells me. "Giving up plastic and making conscious purchases is a privilege. It's good to do, but this is not how we will change the world."

———

The day is painful. Emotional. I feel everything everywhere.

Young people — all volunteers whom I immediately trust — outline the problem and our plan to win.

Climate change is happening.

We have the solutions.

Our government isn't broken. Our government is working just fine — for fossil fuel executives and the ultrarich. Exxon knew about this crisis first. In the 70s they measured the oceans and found that the water was heating. We could have acted then. But they paid our politicians to deregulate. They spent millions on a misinformation campaign telling everyone that we had more time. And then, when it became apparent that the climate crisis was happening, they told everyone that it was too late. That there is nothing we can do. We love oil too much to switch to clean energy.

Politicians on both sides are taking money from the fossil fuel industry.

I am not causing this problem. And I alone cannot solve it.

I am not a bad person. I feel my brain wrap around the idea.

It is difficult to comprehend.

The world is so broken, but we are not helpless. My brain tries to wrap around that, too.

I feel safe in the cage that is trapping me, in this meaningless career that is actively hurting me. This cage is freefalling. And I see that now. Like a magic trick explained. Once you see the string that holds up the floating orb, you cannot un-see it. The illusion is gone.

A cold washes down my body, and I let myself sit in the climate crisis in a way that I never had before. Anxiety. Fear. Anger. Indignation. Acceptance. Hope. Purpose. Direction. I let all the feelings stay, bounce off each other like atoms.

There is nowhere else to go but forward. I feel my brain, my entire body wrap around this.

It is beautiful outside — high seventies, sunny. A tree in the courtyard stretches its green leaves toward the sun.

It is the most beautiful day in the world.

———

Things fizzle out with Trey. I like the script that we have written, but it is not crude enough for him. He wants more dick jokes, profanity. But the main characters are a forty-year-old washed-up professor and a twenty-year-old girl. This pair does not work out.

"I know a producer who is excited about the concept!" he emails me. "I can't pay you anymore, but if you think this has potential, we should keep working on it."

———

I give up entertainment. I stop lying to everyone and myself.

———

"I am doing better," I tell Cheyenne when I see her again. It is the night before my brother's wedding, and we are on an empty dance floor in a hipster bar. She has a new job and new friends. We have been calling each other less, but we both know that we will always be there for one another.

She agrees, "You seem so much happier, Joe."

My aunts, my cousins, my brother, and my grandpa — they all see it too. "You're doing great now!"

Is it that noticeable?

That I hate myself so much less?

———

I find a best friend. The Hallmark girl. Tall and blonde and good at calling out the problems in this world that need to be fixed. Her house in Florida was destroyed by a hurricane – she had to build it back up.

She tells me how her brain works; it is loud and chats endlessly like a nest of hungry birds.

We talk about all the elephants in the room.

———

I delete the apps.

Briefly.

I know that I told Jesse that I would not love again, but this is untrue. I fall in love many times, quickly, all at once. How could I not? I am surrounded by young people who feel what I feel and who are willing to fight for others.

"I am going to cause too much drama and ruin everything," I confess to a stranger at a summit in Berkeley, "I am in love with so many boys at once."

I draw it out for him in Sharpie on a piece of plastic leftover from a takeout container. "This one loves me, but I love this one, and this last boy is cute and nice."

"What is that?" he asks, as I draw a flame.

"An explosion." I heard that cops go undercover and sleep with everyone in social movements to implode them from the inside out.

"You should probably not try to date them all," he tells me. He is right, but I learn the hard way.

———

I accept that my quest for love is inseparable from my demands for justice, and my demands for justice are inseparable from my quest for love. If love is what fuels me, let it fuel me. If I am going to feel the pain of the world, let me act on it.

———

Jesse messages me, infrequently, on Instagram and via text.

Jesse: Have I mentioned lately that I am very grateful that you are doing things and trying to save the world?

Me: That generally annoys me, when people thank me. I want everyone to feel responsible for saving the world.

Jesse: Oh yeah, I am not suggesting that it's not my responsibility too.

Jesse: Just glad someone else is happening.

I feel less dumb about projecting so much on him.

I look at his Instagram. There is a new girl in his photos — a bandmate, a friend? I feel very little. Not jealous. Not curious. A year later, our story already feels like a footnote in the next chapter of my life.

That girl who loved him. She feels like a footnote, too.

I'm not like Jesse. I'm not a nihilist. I am strong and independent and lonely. I am trapped on this dying planet, but I am not trapped alone.

My heart is heavy and my blood pumps through it.

Acknowledgements

There are a lot of people I'd like to thank.

Most notably the people who believed in me when I did not. Thank you, Aaron, for reading (and loving) each draft. Thank you Jenna for advising on my crushes and being a good sport when I cut your character. Thank you Katie and Joule for the incredible notes and feedback. Thank you Sean for being the first person to tell me that this was art — that I could publish this. Thank you Ben and Tory for guiding me through the publishing industry, even though I guided myself out. And thank you Alyza, for always telling me that I am good at writing, especially when I was torn to pieces by peer feedback in our creative writing class.

Mom, in addition to birthing and raising me, thank you for your feedback on the early draft — while it was poorly received at the time, it did make the book much stronger.

Most recently, I'd like to thank Jessica. I'd long given up on publishing my book. The formal publishing industry was too much like the entertainment one and I didn't want to self-publish on Amazon. (Because, well, if it wasn't clear, I hate Amazon.) But after you, a near stranger at the time, told me that my diary made you feel seen — I considered publishing.

Thank you, Grandma Dina and Grandpa Don. Dina for the praise and for the good genes. (You come from a family of Yiddish, leftist, pogrom-surviving-writers — after all. Thank you, ancestors, I might add, for doing some pretty brave shit to get me here.) And thank you Fairy Princess Bubbie Dassi for teaching me the art of storytelling. For telling me that I should sing, that my voice is beautiful.

Thank you, Grandpa Bob, I am glad you got to see your chapter before you died. My Rabbi, Susan Goldberg (who I would also like to thank) told me that when you die your spirit can inhabit other people still on earth, especially if you have unfinished business. I know you are not done having fun. So when I laugh, goose-like, at the pages of this book, I know it is you, laughing too.

Thank you Elif Batuman and adriene maree brown – you do not know me, but your writing (and podcasts) inspire me.

There are others I would just like to thank. Less for this book and more for shaping me into the person I am today. A much less depressed, much less anxious, queer human so happy to be alive each day.

Walker, Alex, Ethan, Ruby, Preston, Jasmin, Ash, David, Monica, and Barbara thank you for bringing me into a movement and showing me that stories can be powerful tools for change. Thank you for naming my gifts. For telling me that everyone has a story to tell. For helping me navigate stepping back and taking up my rightful space. Thank you for the work that you do.

Thank you, Angela, my therapist. You have given me so many tools. Thank you, Dr. Schreider, for the Zoloft. Thank you, Juliet, for showing me that coffee first thing in the morning on an empty stomach is not a great idea. Thank you, Claire, for freeing my voice. And thank you, Cheekface, for giving me a soundtrack to listen to while I edited this book ("Dry Heat/Nice Town" essentially sums up Jesse).

Thank you Charlene for getting me through my 20s. Andrea, thank you for reminding me how to laugh at the absurd and spend money on myself. Cat, thank you for always saying "yes and." Thank you, Jackie, for being my work wife. Thank you Jack and Bailey for teaching me how to be gay. Dan, thank you for getting a dog. Jon, thank you for your fearless reporting. Thank you, Rachel, for showing me there is strength in being sensitive. Thank you Mom and Dad for your brutal honesty and your sense of humor (respectively). Scott, Polly, Kristin, thank you for your decades of friendship and support. Thank you Aunt Rochelle for your kindness, Aunt Amy for always letting me crash at your place even on very little notice. Thank you Camy for inspiring me to play in the woods. And thank you Jonny for existing.

Austin, thank you for showing me how strong a love of friendship can be. For teaching me how to be direct in my communication and how to reject this fucked up society that isn't working for anyone. How to be brave and stand up for what you believe in even if you can't do it perfectly.

Thank you, Kabir, for showing me what a secure romantic relationship can look like with someone who is emotionally available. For being patient with me as I learned to ask for what I need. You taught me that I don't just have to date a musician, I can be one too! I know that I often get upset with you for putting too much pressure on me (I just want to exist and not produce!) but I do appreciate you always reminding me that I am a writer. And thank you for going on tour so I would need a project to do in your absence. I love you. You inspire me.

Lastly, thank you, reader. If you have made it this far, I am beyond flattered. Thank you for reading. I think this makes us friends.

Land Acknowlegment

I would not be here today without the land itself. Griffith Park, especially has gotten me through the last eight years in Los Angeles. This land is native land, Tongva land. I am a guest here and a steward. As such, I have set up a Kuuyam Nahwá'a (guest exchange) with the Tonga Taraxat Paxaavxa Conservancy (TPPC). I have set up monthly contributions to the TPPC and will be donating a portion of my proceeds from this book.

About the Author

Nicole Levin has been published in the *Harvard Lampoon*, *New Yorker Shouts*, *ATTN:*, and most importantly, *KNOCK.LA*. She currently lives in Los Angeles with her musician partner and her dog Nina. She spends most of her time puzzling, dancing, and organizing to phase out urban oil drilling in Los Angeles.